TRAIL CROSSING
SIXTEEN COUNTIES

Advance Praise for
Trail Crossing Sixteen Counties

"Erwin's work operates on the same emotional wavelength as Cheever, Carver, and Salinger, with stories that examine and plunge into the deepest layers of our beautiful, flawed humanity." **R.J. Fox, author** *Love & Vodka: My Surreal Adventures in the Ukraine and Awaiting Identification*

"Gary James Erwin's stories capture a side of life not often acknowledged in the wider world. He shines a light into the gritty darkness of everyday people and lets his characters sparkle like diamonds." **Peter Barlow, author of** *Little Black Dots*

"Gary James Erwin writes stories of pain, life, loss and childhood, tales that take place in and around Detroit and in the small towns of northern Michigan. He crafts his stories using strong images that will put the reader in each of the scenes he creates. His detailing is rich and complete, and readers will feel the themes rising up from his imagery to make a very human connection. Intriguing stories that rate worthy of reading again and again." **M. L. Liebler, author and editor of** *I Want to Be Once, Heaven Was Detroit: Essays on Detroit Music from Jazz to Hip Hop* **(both Wayne State University Press) and the new anthology** *R=E=S=P=E=C=T: Poems about Detroit Music* **(Michigan State University Press).**

For my wife Julie,
and our kids, Zac, Olivia and Sam.

Trail Crossing Sixteen Counties

Stories By

GARY JAMES ERWIN

Adelaide Books
New York / Lisbon
2019

TRAIL CROSSING SIXTEEN COUNTIES
short stories
by Gary James Erwin

Published by Adelaide Books, New York / Lisbon
adelaidebooks.org

Editor-in-Chief
Stevan V. Nikolic

For any information, please address Adelaide Books
at info@adelaidebooks.org
or write to:
Adelaide Books
244 Fifth Ave. Suite D27
New York, NY, 10001

ISBN13: 978-1-951214-06-7
ISBN10: 1-951214-06-4

Printed in the United States of America

Contents

What power has love but forgiveness?

William Carlos Williams

When the jealousy fades away
And it's ash and dust for cash and lust
And it's just hallelujah
And love in thoughts and love in the words
Love in the songs they sing in the church
And no hard feelings

The Avette Brothers

Transposed

After my mother's cardiac arrest, she returned to her studio in the basement, determined to paint again. Each day she sat smoking Winston Ultra Lights, her eyes narrowed against the smoke as she peered blankly at the stacks of incomplete canvasses that lay on an angle against the far wall. Her appearance didn't convey the disturbance in vascular composition that her mind and body had recently endured. Her hair was still long and blond. Her skin smooth. Eyes blue, translucent like the ocean. She'd begun to hum— mostly slogans from television ads or passages from the bible as she drifted around the house, a paint brush pinched between her fingers like a cigar, searching the walls for pieces of her early artwork that suddenly required revision.

Within a few days of being home, she'd located her blue painting robe draped over the metal folding chair behind the basement staircase, and she began to wear it in earnest every day. It was frayed at the elbows, the fabric consumed by the scents of oil paint, turpentine, and Channel Number Five. Despite the heart problems and attendant shifts in chemistry, her skin still retained the pungency of her art, one of the few characteristics that would never change: in the months before and after she came home, she often made ham sandwiches on wheat bread for lunch, which tasted faintly of turpentine no matter how much mustard she applied.

Sometimes I worked in the opposite corner of our cluttered basement, hidden by the dusty walls of the aluminum furnace, rerouting two spurs of bumper track on my model railroad as she labored quietly over her latest project: a splintering wood picture frame, onto which she'd tacked an assortment of multi-colored Christmas bows using my father's hydraulic staple gun; a white plastic kitchen garbage can, spattered with mountainous globs of green, red and blue oil paint; or an arrangement of silk roses spray-painted gold to match the family photograph that hung on an angle above the fireplace in the front room. None of these pieces compared to what she'd produced prior to her illness: oil paintings of textured mountain landscapes, veined with rivers that glinted in sunlight; charcoal illustrations of my father swinging his driver in the vacant field next door at dusk, the pitch between light and shadow evenly balanced throughout the drawing; ink compositions of my sisters and I, mounted inside oak and pine frames carved from trees she and my father had cut up north from our property in Mancelona County years earlier.

The quality in her early work was abundant and we became aware of it at a young age: her paintings and drawings were often among the first items sold during our town's annual weekend-long sidewalk sale just before Labor Day, earning as much as one-hundred dollars a piece. On occasion, she took orders for the following season, jotting neighbors' requests into a tiny spiral notebook she kept tucked in the breast pocket of her paint-spattered robe. But some years the attendance wasn't high. To promote her work during those lean weekends, my sisters and I walked around the labyrinth of white cement sidewalks downtown, past the stained glass windows of Our Lady of Victory Catholic Church and brick facades of NBD Bank and the D & C, displaying color Polaroids of her work to people eating spaghetti and drinking wine at Genopolis' outdoor Italian café. Sometimes we had luck soliciting the parents who stood at the teetering railing of Ford Field at the south end of town, smoking cigarettes and peering down from the street at their dust-covered little leaguers warming up for a game. We required little reward for our efforts: cheeseburgers, fries and chocolate malts from Burger Chef or double scoops of chocolate chip ice cream on sugar cones from Cloverdale Deli downtown.

"Don't get used to this," she often warned my sisters and I as our station wagon barreled through the tree-covered lanes and down the dusty county roads on our way to eat, a lit cigarette pinched between her middle and index finger of her right hand, "this is okay once in a while." As she drove, her fingers tapped against the steering wheel in time with the Credence Clearwater Revival eight-track tape that usually blared on the car radio, interrupted only when she claimed, "French fries and shakes can't replace your mother's home cooking."

When she said this, Sara, Ann and I would snicker at each other, making sure Mom could see us in the rear view mirror. Based on experience and lack of gourmet expertise, her culinary skills required refinement, a fact we often teased her about.

But after her hospital stay, nothing was the same. Her fingers trembled incessantly, making it impossible to write her name. The medication prescribed by her doctors caused her to fall asleep in her studio chair, her head slung against her chest, a lit cigarette sandwiched between her thumb and forefinger like a pencil as the smoke uncurled near the basement windows. If I didn't pinch it out in the MSU shot glass next to her table that overflowed with lipstick smeared butts, she would have ended up on fire at least a dozen times. Some days she even forgot our names and peered at us with a glassy look in her eyes, as if we were strangers who suddenly strode in off the street and collapsed on the couch and easy chair in front of the family room television. Eventually the town council rented her sale booth to Mr. James, a retired General Motors engineer who sold hand-crafted wicker baskets, wine holders and clear glass bottles of homemade beer.

She must have known that she would never be the same after her arrest. To combat her bouts of sudden unconsciousness, confusion and artistic despair since her return, she'd shift my sister's rust-infested Duster into neutral, coast backwards down our sloped driveway with the stolen keys in the ignition, and floor it to the Plymouth Hilton, something she hadn't done before she got sick. Once there, I envisioned her sitting at the dimly lit hotel bar in her blond wig, sipping whiskey and 7 Ups, and flirting with the drunk executives from Ford or GM who strayed in for happy hour following unsatisfactory outings at the local country club, their golf shirts dark with sweat. When my father arrived home from the bank and trudged into the house from the garage door, tilted his wide nose toward the ceiling of the kitchen and discovered the absence of cigarette smoke in the air, he'd clench his eyes shut and mutter a faint, "Goddamnit." Then he'd cram his fingers into the front pocket of his suit pants, extract two wads of crumpled dollar bills, and drop them into the lap of my sister Sara, who sat with her best friend Karen on the leather couch in the family room, their legs draped over each arm as they watched General Hospital.

"Go get Mom," he would say, handing her his heavy key ring. "Probably at the Hilton again. Pizza here when you get back."

"Right now? Can we go after this is over?" Sara begged, squirming at the untenable sense of helplessness she must have felt toward his assignment.

My father would move in front of the television, blocking their view, his large hairy hands planted firmly on his hips.

"You need to go now, before she drinks too much. There's an extra five in it if you leave now."

"Can I go?" I often asked.

"No," my father would bark, his usual refrain. "Maybe when you're older. Not today."

In most instances, Sara gave her share of the money to Karen. I never questioned why she did this: after her return from the bar, Mom sometimes grew incomprehensibly hostile toward all of us, revealing glimpses of the exasperation we'd lived with before her illness. We never had much warning: even though her new medication had softened her disposition considerably, her moods still made our stomachs nervous and caused grainy fragments of bile to rise in our throats whenever we'd done something that made her angry. But Mom liked Karen; this fact was not lost on my sister.

Sometimes I followed them into the garage and watched them pull away, left to imagine Karen as she unfolded her long tan legs from the passenger side, stepped out and glided into the smoky bar. In my mind, I often saw her reappearing at the doorway with Mom to escort her outside, their feet scrunching as they moved slowly across the stone lot. Once they were within five feet of the car, I could see Mom take a final drag on her cigarette, spit out the butt and address Sara through clenched teeth, hissing under her breath, "How dare you treat me like a child! I'm your mother!"

"I know," Sara might murmur, arms wrapped tightly around her ribs, forehead creased with uncertainty and shame for having to retrieve Mom yet again. "But we're all worried about you."

"I don't care. I'm your goddamn mother!" Mom would rasp as smoke seeped from her nostrils.

Then she'd slump into the front seat with a grunt, her wig tipped slightly askew, the stench of whiskey wafting into the car after her. Sometimes, as I watched both cars turn into our driveway from my bedroom window, I saw Sara and Mom staring sullenly at the untended Austrian Pines and weed-infested rosebushes in our front yard, perhaps embittered with humiliation as they silently tried to comprehend the difference between this life and the one our family had lived before.

Indian Pond

She smelled of paper and dust. Maybe a hint of oil paint, too. An oily film was smudged across the upper right corner of the cover and made the white letters and numbers of June 1969 look faded. Adam rubbed his chin and squinted through the tent blackness, past the featureless faces of his friends, trying to calculate his age when this issue came out: six, maybe seven—a good five years before his mother got sick the first time.

He bent his head to the magazine and took another whiff. He liked to smell the girl on the cover, to touch her with his cheek, his eyelids and his nose, to press his lips to the dusty pages until it felt as if he were going to sneeze. He never wanted to stop sniffing.

He settled the magazine into his lap. His flashlight, dangling loosely in his fingertips, moved when he breathed and made white lines of light squiggle across the page like fluorescent snakes that crawled around her cascading red mane. With his pinky he traced her figure and wondered what it would be like to have her naked body sprawled on the tent floor in front of them at this very minute, what he would do if he had the chance to kiss and probe the secrete parts of her body that the photograph didn't reveal. She wouldn't smell like paint or dust in real life. Apples or oranges maybe, but not paint, not that odor that stung his eyes whenever he glided down the basement stairs in his house to see what painting his mother was working on. He couldn't imagine the girl's soft breasts or the smooth ticklish spot around her belly button smelling like that, or her hair and fingers giving off any bad odor. Those parts smelled natural; those parts reminded him of wild flowers that shot up through the brown stalks of field grass in the spring and swayed back and forth along the shore of Indian Pond when freight trains clattered past.

He bent his head to the page and breathed heavily until blood rushed to his temples and made his face hot. "She's the one," he said and smoothed the crinkled page with his palms, then raised the magazine to show his two friends as the flashlight beam swam across her figure.

He looked back down at her, then closed his eyes and envisioned every detail of her face and every contour of her smooth body. She was one of his favorites, pulled from the dislocated mounds of *Sports Illustrateds* and *National Geographics* in the basement one blistering morning after his father left early for the doctor's office. Now that his mother was in the hospital again, Adam kept a magazine wedged between his *Monopoly* and Life games in his bedroom closet, and one rolled up inside his G.I. Joe Command Center, places he wouldn't normally hide them if she were around. The other magazines he'd stashed in different parts of the house: a willowy brunette pinched between the wall and couch in the basement, a small black mole hovering just above the left corner of her gaping mouth; a blonde stuffed under the mattress of his bed, her red fingernails barely touching her lower lip as she lolled on the sandy shore of an island choked with palm trees. Sometimes he imagined them standing above him as he lay in the tall orchard grass watching the billows of clouds lumber by and feeling himself growing hard, the soft hairs on their arms and finely molded faces beading with a dewy perspiration he wanted to taste on his lips.

He traced the girl's face and neck in the magazine with his finger, then squirmed a few seconds, trying to fit his shorts around his erection without having to touch it in front of his friends. "What I'd do if she were here right now," Adam whispered, looking up at Johnny and Ed, the magazine propped up in front of him and the flashlight beam focused more steadily on her body so they could see which girl he was talking about.

He was twelve. He played baseball in fields overgrown with barbed weeds and liked to watch movies about the bloody collapse of Hitler's regime during World War II. Each morning he counted the hard, crunchy brown hairs that had begun to emerge in his armpits using tweezers and the bathroom mirror. He cherished the cool taste of an ice cream sandwich on a humid summer day while he hiked back through the orchard to his side of the township as plump, black cicadas screeched in the tree crowns above.

On Saturdays he fished with his father to forget. It was a distraction they tailored around his mother's stays at the hospital as the days crept deeper into the hot summer and made big drops of sweat fall from their brows. They caught fish—some of notable size—but at these they only smiled and marveled without speaking, raising them toward the sun to study their working gills, then tossing them back into the dark water and watching them swim past clouds of lake weeds and disappear.

They spent most of their time beneath the hazy layers of humidity that clung to trees and floated above the pond, listening to the swells of water that lapped against the sides of the boat. Eventually, maybe near sundown, raccoons wandered down to the mossy edge and skimmed the water with their paws, hunting for the young fish that drifted like shadows among the fallen tree trunks and dead stumps that sat half submerged in the shallows. Sometimes the coons caught fish. When they did, their chattering voices carried across the water to the boat where Adam and his father sat, searching for fish feeding on the water bugs that skated back and forth across the glassy surface. They stared for hours in silence, until the 9 p.m. freight train clattered around the valley ledge, its big white letters "SOO LINE" fogged with rust as it thundered past.

"Well, I guess that means it's about time," his father would murmur.

A heaviness settled in Adam's chest when his father turned away and watched the train claw into the setting sun—a dampness that clung to his lungs and encumbered him with a drowsiness that made his eyes sag and his veins feel as if they'd been filled with sap instead of blood. He never wanted to leave. Months ago, when his mother got sick that first time, he sat on the front porch all day long with his face in his hands staring out at East Chigwooden and searching the small dark cracks in the cement for something that would make him cry. No matter how hard he tried, he couldn't coax the tears to come—not even when he thought of all those clear tubes plugged into her arms and chest or imagined her sitting by the window after visiting hours were over with no one to talk to except her dim reflection in the glass. Maybe, when she sat alone gazing at the yellow lights in downtown Ann Arbor, she searched her past for the debris of family illness that no one had ever talked about, trying to piece together the reason for her condition, as if it lay somewhere between the light and the dark outside her window.

"I think Uncle Morris had it in '79," she whispered to Adam and his father one Sunday when they came for a visit. "The same kind of angina. But he was older. I'm still fairly young, so that's in my favor. It just takes a little time."

"What's it feel like, Mom?"

She turned and touched his knee as he sat on the bed beside her. "Do you really want to know, honey?" she asked, smoothing her hand over his leg and looking into his eyes. "It's hard to describe, but I'll try if you really want to know."

"Maybe you should rest," his father cut in, standing up from the chair at the foot of her bed. He came forward and leaned on the end railing, then beamed down at her, the fine lines around his eyes growing more pronounced when he smiled. "Might not be such a good idea to tell him right now. All that technical mumbo-jumbo is pretty confusing."

"It's okay," she said and nodded. "He's old enough to get the picture. He should learn what's going on."

"Lyn, he's just a boy. You don't really expect him to understand. Even I had a hard time trying to get what the doctor was saying."

"He should know," she said, her soft voice growing breathless. "Besides, being 'just a boy' doesn't mean he can't know something about his health history." She took some deep breaths and closed her eyes. "I suspect that if I knew before this happened, it may not have happened at all. He should know what to look out for," she whispered, "that's all."

"Really, now," Dad said, "I don't think it's.... appropriate."

His mother raised her hand to him. "It's not a question of what is and isn't appropriate. It's about being well and not feeling sick." She opened her eyes, put her head back against her pillow and looked wearily at Adam's father. "I think he should know, James. It's about us—him, me, you—the family. We should make him understand."

"How?" his father asked. "I mean—what's he gonna know?" He took a few steps away from the bed and raised his hands, as if weighing the question in his meaty palms. "All I'm saying is that it might not be such a good idea trying to explain it right now. Maybe later, when you're home, but not now. He'll get confused."

"I can help him understand," she said flatly. "In fact, this hospital room is probably the best place for him to learn."

Adam looked at his mother's hand resting on his knee. It was small in comparison to his leg, just a bony thing with pale skin and small blue veins stretched tightly over the knuckles and long fingers. Chips of brown and red oil paint flecked the oval portions of her nails, and the thin, smooth ridges of bone on the back of her palm rose and fell when she moved her fingers over his knee cap.

"That's okay," he said, enjoying the feel of her palm moving back and forth over his knee, watching the different colors of old paint on her nails blend into one hue. "Maybe you'd better sleep."

His father leaned over her once again. "Rest," he whispered. "you should sleep. We can talk about it later." He patted her hand, then bent down and softly kissed it.

The afternoon following that visit, Adam sat on the porch and tried to summon the tears, but nothing worked. He squeezed his lids with his fingers, slapped the side of his face a dozen or so times until he could feel the heat radiating from his red flesh, but all he felt was an intense, burning sensation inside his stomach and on his cheek. After a while his father walked up behind him, his feet making slow, measured steps on the creaking wood floor, then stopped.

"Your Mom's a strong woman. She'll be all right," he said from behind the screen door, trying to sound optimistic. "I know I've said it at least a dozen times, but I feel it to be true. She'll get better and be home before you know it."

"I know," Adam mumbled, rubbing his dry sockets with his fists, then looking up at the street as a dusty pick up drifted past. When he was ten or eleven, she used to sit with him on the porch after dinner showing him how to sketch the slope of their front lawn and the infrequent cars that passed in her pad using a dark-leaded pencil. He would lean in close to her and allow her paint-speckled fingers to guide his hand over the page, until an exact likeness of their yard and dirt road emerged on the paper.

He looked down at his hand now, then moved it across his lap, trying to recall the drawing movements she'd taught him. It had been a long time since he felt the dryness of her hand on his. He wondered what it would be like not to feel that again, or to have her around for any length of time, what he would do if he had the house to himself every afternoon the rest of his life. Growing up, he liked watching her glide silently from room to room, her robe stained with the same colors of paint that dotted her fingernails—red, blue, green, brown, and some other shades he didn't know the names of. When she waltzed into the kitchen to fix his lunch, the scent of oil paint always followed in her wake. No matter how vigorously she scrubbed her hands, his ham and cheese sandwiches always tasted like paint after he took his first bite. But after so many years, those sandwiches never really tasted right if he couldn't detect the slightest hint of oil paint in them.

"She'll be okay, right?" Adam asked, turning around to look at his father.

"Of course," his father said, his lean body shadowed by the screen door. "I suspect sooner than we think. She's a quick healer."

Adam nodded, then looked back out over the field. He wasn't sure that what his father had said was the truth, but that was all right. Maybe he could wait for some kind of strength to unfurl or suddenly dawn on him one day as he sat on the banks of Indian Pond when he was feeling alone, peering at his muddied reflection on the water. Eventually, he told himself, he would be strong for the both of them.

He loved his father. He loved that part of him that fished for comfort in the murky water of Indian Pond as he gazed over the edge of the boat and stared at the reflection of his face. When they fished together they sometimes talked about the prospects of the Lions, whispering about Billy Sims' break-away speed as their boat drifted silently past the moss-covered trunks that littered the shore and finally stopped in the green muck at the north end of the pond where frogs could be heard clucking below the shafts of willows.

They talked to forget his mother's illness, trying to bury it beneath the sound of their voices echoing against the trees in some corners of the pond, or disappearing over the water without ever reaching the opposite shore. After a few hours in the boat, their talk thinned into complaints about the steamy weather and the things that needed repair on the house, like the aluminum shutters dented from a recent hail storm, or the small doors to the storage cabinets in the garage that cracked when his mother backed the station wagon into them after a trip to the grocery store. But in the quiet moments Adam felt the weight of his father's unspoken worries linger in the air above them like the threat of rain as they rowed quietly toward the shore just before sunset.

A warm, sweet pain blossomed in his groin the summer that he turned twelve—a spot of discomfort that flowed through his inner thighs and ebbed on days he and his father fished together. He remembered his mother and tried not to think about the girls in his magazines. Instead, he imagined the bloated green bullfrogs he and his friends shot with a BB gun on the shore of Indian Pond, their bodies heaped at the edge of the water, sunlight glinting off their moist backs. But even these thoughts failed him. Eventually he found himself in the basement surrounded by all her paintings, feeling the pages of a magazine crinkle and rip just below his face as his body rocked back and forth.

After a month or two the feeling began to fade. It came mostly in the afternoon—sharp, distinct, it's range confined to his inner thighs and lower stomach as the wetness flowed into his shorts and glued the waist band of his Fruit-Of-The Looms to his skin. It smelled like bleach. No matter how hard he tried not to inhale that smell, he still caught traces of it on his clothing or in his hands when he went outside to play baseball with his friends. After a month he told himself that he wouldn't do it anymore, that it wasn't right, but this didn't work: each day he still found himself downstairs stretched out on the couch with his head pressed firmly to the coarse fabric below his face, his eyes fixed on the specks of dust that floated in the beams of sunlight that streamed down a few inches in front of his mother's painting cove.

Adam clung to his side of the tent and stared at his friends giggling into their magazines, their heads cocked down, flashlights shifting from page to page. He moved to his right, poked his head out the doorway and looked up at the sky speckled with thousands of stars.

He wondered if anyone could see him. Maybe, from a grassy hilltop above town or staring out the window of a slow moving jet, someone could see his gaze glued to the starry sky above him, and the ribbons of his neck muscles straining as he thought about all those afternoons in the basement. He considered the possibility that he may have left a magazine out or other piece of evidence of what he'd done: the corner of his pillow jutting out from under the couch; a page, accidentally ripped from his magazine, crumpled on the last step of the staircase; the tag from his undershorts resting on the floor in a pool of warm sunlight. Perhaps, before that bad bout had gripped his mother a month ago and left her struggling for breath on the back lawn, she'd found his pillow while arranging the dozens of half-finished paintings and unused canvasses that lay against the walls and rested in piles near the couch. Or his father, hunting around the basement for a tackle box or old pole, had nudged the couch aside with his knee and discovered the pillow himself.

Adam shook his head, trying to rid himself of these images. If caught, he could never look into his parents' faces without feeling dirty, as if a clean part of his innocence had unleashed itself, spilled out through a seam in his body, and left him half the boy they thought he was. Sometimes at night, when he finished saying his prayers and gazed through the dark at his window, watching the moonlight spill across the glass, he imagined his mother's smile fade after discovering his magazines. Or else he saw her trembling, paint-smeared fingers carefully pinching a worn end of his pillow and raising it towards the stairway light for inspection some late afternoon while he sat along the banks of Indian Pond, looking through a magazine.

He couldn't really picture his father's reaction; with his mother in the hospital, he'd become distant and remote, as if her illness lay heavy on his mind every second he watched a Tiger game in the den or sat hunched over the kitchen table in the late afternoon, squinting impatiently at the three -day-old newspaper spread in front of him. Adam shook his head, then looked up at the sky, at the soft white rings that encompassed the moon, and wondered what he would say if they both caught him lying on the basement couch in the middle of a hot afternoon.

He brought his head back into the tent and looked over at his friend Ed, sitting Indian-style across from him. Ed laid his magazine down and listened to the crickets in the grass just outside the tent door. He was short, with fine straight hair the color of field grass and puffy eyelids that drooped over his pupils.

Behind Ed, smothering a cigarette against the sole of his tennis shoe, loomed Johnny Hazleton, a new boy who'd moved with his mother to town from South Chicago earlier in the year. He was two years older than Ed and Adam; this fact fascinated Ed beyond reason, as if Johnny had garnished some worldly experience Ed wasn't privy to. To Adam, it seemed that the world in which Johnny had once lived found him and his mother unsuitable for its taste and coughed them out into this remote county of Michigan.

"Look at this one," Johnny muttered, his voice gravelly from cigarettes. He dropped his magazine in the middle of the three of them as they sat inside the tent, then waved the flashlight across the page. A dark-skinned man with thick knots of black hair plastered all over his chest appeared, stretched out on a carpet of white sand. A blond woman had her head hunkered down into his crotch.

"Is she doing what I think she's doing?" Ed asked, leaning forward to get a better view.

"Blow job," Johnny murmured. "You guys know what that is?"

Adam nodded. Ed sat back.

Johnny shifted his head back and forth mechanically. "Kind of neat, the way it feels," he murmured, looking down at his magazine.

"You ever have it done?" Adam asked.

"Sure. Back in Chicago, an old girlfriend used to do it all the time whenever I needed it. Really feels good."

"What's it feel like?" Ed asked.

Johnny leaned back. "Well," he began, his tiny eyes darting across the tent floor. "It's like a vacuum, except that it feels soft and doesn't hurt at all. My girlfriend was really good at it."

After a moment he peered through the darkness of the tent at Ed and then at Adam. "She told me I was big," he announced.

"Big...," Adam repeated, a little annoyed at the encroaching story.

Johnny put his magazine down and looked across the tent at Adam and Ed

"You wanna see it?" Johnny whispered. He looked over at Ed, then back to Adam. He slid his body to the tent center and ran his tongue over his lips. Saliva made them sparkle in the moonlight that shone through the door flap. "I kinda had the feeling you both did. Just ask me and I'll show ya."

"Right," Adam muttered, looking back down at his magazine, feeling uneasy at how fast Johnny was willing to expose his crotch.

"Just admit it and I'll be happy to show you."

"You're sick, Johnny," Ed said.

Johnny pressed his fists to the ground, levitated himself forward a few more inches towards Adam, and then stood up.

"Keep your pants on, Johnny," Ed said. "No one cares."

"You'll get your chance, Sanders," Johnny whispered, tracing his belt with a finger. "Just be patient."

"Stop pigboy," Ed chuckled, "no one wants to see it. Maybe your mom makes you keep it at home when you go out. Maybe your dad can take it off, like a car tire."

Ed and Adam looked at each other, then exploded with laughter. They rocked back and forth a few seconds, clutching their sides. As Johnny knelt between them, Adam recalled rumors about Johnny's father leaving him and his mother before moving to town, but they were nothing he could substantiate. Johnny kneeled before them, his mouth formed into a small pout, his gaze shifting nervously between Adam and Ed.

"I know one thing," Johnny roared above the laughter, his lower lip quivering. "Rickson here does want to see it."

Adam and Ed continued laughing.

"Funny, huh," Johnny yelled. "Tell ya what, Rickson. To make you happy, I will show it to you." He stood again and began fumbling with his pants button.

Ed put his magazine down. "Jeez, Johnny," he chuckled, "we were just kidding. Enough already. Are you a fag or something?"

But Johnny kept going, until the white of his under shorts was visible against his pale skin.

Johnny clutched a wad of underwear and jeans. He moved forward until he was within an arm's length of Adam. "Okay, you ready," Johnny said. "Here we go. On three. One. Two. Three!"

Adam slid back and looked away. A few seconds passed. Finally Ed said, "Adam, he's not doing it."

"What a wuss," Johnny cried. "God, Rickson, I was just kidding. Wasn't gonna make you jealous by showing it off. I swear, you can be such a wuss."

Adam looked up. "Your dad teach you that one?" he shot back, shaking his head. He glanced at Ed sitting quietly across the tent, then at Johnny, who turned away suddenly embarrassed and began fumbling blindly for his pants buckle. Adam wondered what he would have done if Johnny had actually exposed himself—what he would have said or how he would have felt. Giving Johnny a straight right to the jaw seemed the appropriate thing to do, but the results could be hazardous, given Johnny's age and size. A feeling of uncertainty made Adam's head swim, and the space inside the tent began to grow fuzzy and undefined. He gazed at Johnny standing in front of him, chuckling. Then Adam rolled his magazine up with his sleeping bag and stood up.

"Adam, come on, don't leave," Ed pleaded. "He didn't mean it, right Johnny?"

Adam brushed past Johnny. "Of course not," he whispered, turning away from Adam as he left the tent.

He draped his sleeping bag over his shoulder and walked home with his flashlight on, past the yellow shreds of daisies that littered the spaces between houses, their crowns chopped off by lawn mowers and scattered over yards like confetti from a parade. He lumbered through a thick haze that hovered above the water in the Gliders' front ditch, then cut across a back yard studded with small dirt pyramids made by moles. Finally he reached his house, crept to the side door and slowly opened it. He slipped into the laundry room and glided past a yellow basket overflowing with sheets, dish towels, his father's tee shirts and Adam's cut-off shorts. Another basket, filled with the same sort of laundry, stood on top of the dryer.

He wandered through the front hallway, past his parents' room where his father breathed heavily in his sleep, then to the basement door. He opened it, reached above his head, pulled the fish string that turned on the bulb, and followed the tunnel of yellow light downstairs to his mother's painting cove. When he got to the bottom, he put his hands forward, felt for the stool, and sat down.

He turned and gazed up at the window behind him. A splotch of green velvety mold grew on the glass above her canvasses and mingled with the cottony threads of spider webs woven into elaborate patterns among the rafters. He turned back around and peered into the areas of the basement where everything from his family's past hid in the dark beneath dusty blankets or packed into cardboard boxes. The only time he came downstairs was to be alone with his magazines, and even those moments were brief and sweaty interludes during the day; he was always in a hurry, working feverishly to avoid sudden detection. Still, his father, at least from what Adam knew, hadn't been in the basement for months.

He peered at the area where the couch sat, then walked towards it. Once there, he stretched out on his stomach and thought about Johnny. He thought about Ed and how Johnny got him to do anything he wanted. His only best friend had been sucked in by the countless Johnny-stories that had to be untrue. Adam took a deep breath. Thinking of Johnny made him sweat—it beaded along the small of his back and slid down into his shorts. He decided he was going to get back at Johnny. No real pain—no blows to his head, stomach or chest. Images would be enough.

He closed his eyes and imagined Johnny's mother as a young woman strewn on the couch beneath his body, her skin as white as porcelain, legs splayed. Her breasts, tummy, even the patch of brown hair on her crotch were like fertile islands that gave expression to her face, one that replaced the leathery-looking woman he saw slouched in a lawn chair on the back porch of Johnny's house that first day he and Ed had met her. She slugged whiskey from a Flintstones cartoon glass all day long and basted herself in suntan oil until her skin, dented and bunched together in fleshy deposits around her thighs and upper arms, looked as soft and brown as peanut butter.

Adam imagined her lips fluttering as he drew closer to her and felt her hot breath curling around his nose and mouth. He could taste the saltiness of her skin on her neck, behind her ears and on her cheeks. He stuck his fingers between the wall and couch and extracted one of his magazines. He spread it out in front of him, but because of the dark, he had to angle it towards a patch of light thrown from the bulb at the top of the stairs. The somber, curtained eyes of a long brunette lying on a cot came into focus. Posters of red Mustangs and black El Caminoes covered the wall behind her.

"Well, hello," he whispered, his fingers digging deeper into the space between the couch and wall, searching for his pillow. He closed his eyes and thought of Johnny's mother, but as his fingers probed the area between him and the wall, he felt the coarse texture of a canvass just below the spot where he usually stashed his pillow. He squeezed his arm further down to gain a better grip on it, then pulled upwards and freed the painting from its resting spot.

In the dark, with specks of stairway light barely freckling this side of the basement where other unfinished canvasses lay scattered, this painting looked like a patch of several colors mixed together—orange, powder blue, green, brown, red. Weeping willows huddled around the glassy water and beyond them stood oak trees with crowns lit by autumn colors. Beneath one of the willows sat a crudely painted figure with its hands coupled in its lap. He or she, Adam couldn't tell which, wore a red and white striped shirt and black pants. But there wasn't any expression on the face—no eyes, mouth or nose, just a smear of creamy paint framed by a sprinkle of dark hair. Adam couldn't understand it. His mother had never before mentioned seeing Indian Pond or ever walking out to the orchard to look at it; yet here it was, locked onto the canvass by her imagination, the art of her brush strokes unblemished by the absence of this person's face.

"How?" he grunted. He stared up at the wood beams.

When did she go there? Why? He closed his eyes. Is this me? he wondered, looking again at the unfinished figure in the painting and smoothing a finger over it. Inside he felt an anger grow, a tight squeezing of muscle in his chest that constricted his breath. She should have said that she'd been there, he thought to himself. He threw the magazine toward the stairway where it landed in a wedge of light at the foot of the stairs. He made a fist. He held it above him so long that the blood drained from his fingers and made his hand tingle. Finally he brought it down hard against his thigh once, then twice until he feel forward onto his knees in despair, his body landing on top of some canvasses. The frames at the end of the couch smacked the ground; the painting slipped from his lap and settled beside him. He pushed a hand out, touched it, then felt tears on his cheek. Within seconds he heard the creak of his father's bare footsteps near his bedroom, then at the basement entrance. The door opened and the light clicked on.

"Adam?" his father called. Adam quickly wiped his cheek and watched his father's shadow sway back and forth on the floor, then move forward until it enveloped the magazine resting in a heap at the foot of the stairs. The shadow concealed the brunette's naked body as his father descended the stairway.

"Adam." The brass screws that secured the wood railing moaned as his father leaned his weight onto it. "Come here, son," his father said somberly.

Adam peered at the crumbs of paper, wood, and minute drops of oil paint that lay on the floor before him like fragments of an imaginary world that had somehow teetered off its axis and collapsed into the dark basement where it shattered into millions of pieces. He raised himself up, looked into the area of the basement where the furnace sat, at his mother's painting cove, then dropped his head to the cool floor.

"Come on, boy. Time for bed," his father cooed. He moved forward a few feet, then stopped. He cleared his throat, and in a small, feeble voice he said, "We'll go fishing in the morning if you want. Should be good day for it—weatherman says it's gonna rain. Maybe we can head up north to the cabin this weekend, get a start on that blind and drop some bait."

Adam swallowed and licked his lips. After a few seconds his father walked over and knelt down beside him, then laid a palm softly on his back and rubbed. "Come on son, it's getting late."

But Adam didn't move. He simply stayed on the ground for what seemed to him a long time, moving a finger back and forth across the rough texture of that faceless figure resting against a tree in his mother's rendition of Indian Pond.

Exchange of Words

We'd recognized the discrepancies in her speech the third day after admission.

"Mouth stick," she'd murmured one morning during a brief period of consciousness. She raised her limp hand, then pointed a crooked finger at a tube of lipstick resting among the items of her makeup bag that my sisters had scattered across the bedside table. She cocked her head toward my father and squinted as he stood next to her with his hand on her shoulder, his blond eyebrows raised in question.

"Here," mom instructed him, her blue eyes bloodshot and glazed, a finger delicately probing her cracked and dry lips. She puffed air into her cheeks to extend her lips outward, an exercise that immediately drained the blood from her face and caused her eyelids to flutter. My father reached across her body but before he could snatch her lipstick, the IV machine chirped, her hand fell heavily to the bed and she'd slipped into another drug-induced sleep. When she inhaled, a gurgling sound gushed from her throat and nose, as if gravel shifted somewhere inside her nasal cavity.

"Red meat, cigarettes, genetics, stress," her doctor speculated in response to my father's inquiry concerning the reasons for her unexpected heart problems, given her relatively young age of 42. The doctor leaned over her as she slept and pressed his stethoscope to her chest. "Might be one or a combination of them all," he continued. "We'll know more in a week or two. When she's able, you may want to think about taking some time away go somewhere relaxing."

With his eyes closed, the doctor turned his head and listened to the ebb of blood as it flowed to and from her heart, over the fatty deposits that had conspired against her the last ten years of her life. It was the eighth examination of my mother he'd conducted within four days. His perplexity in calculating the extent to which her heart had seized up was evident in the scrutiny of his pinched eyes and bouts of silence. In the middle of his first analysis a day or two after she was admitted, Mom woke unexpectedly to discover him leaning over her, his dark-skinned face inches from her nose. She shot a fist toward his jaw, her knuckles glancing off his bearded chin.

"Son of a bitch in my clothes," she garbled, glaring into his startled face.

This was the mother we were accustomed to living with our entire life, a striking contrast to the morning we found her slumped over the clothes dryer in the laundry room after breakfast, her eyes rolled up so that only the whites were visible, a ball of sweat socks clenched in her fist. But sometimes the contradictions were difficult to comprehend and without evidence: before she became ill, she attended to our collective and individual needs carefully, often making three different dishes at dinner for my sisters and me, or scheduling days in which only she and my sisters or I went to lunch together downtown. My family and I sat next to her bed that second day in the hospital with our mouths open, bolstered by the speed and agility she was able to marshal toward the doctor given the gravity of her affliction. Not once in the years prior to her heart condition did she ever display any degree of athleticism.

Each time he came into her room after that day, I watched his uneasy gaze shift back and forth behind his wire-rimmed glasses and survey the rise and fall of her chest, an observation I found unsettling. His thick, wiry black beard rose high on his cheeks and obscured his lips, which made it difficult to determine their precise location when he wasn't speaking. By the fourth day the invisibility of his mouth undermined my confidence in him: when he turned and addressed us, it looked as if his words were issued from two horizontal strips of coarse black hair. My sister Ann and I called him Dr. Hair. One night after our visit, she leaned across the back seat of our car as we silently drove home, cupped her freckled hands around her mouth and whispered in my ear, "When Dr. Hair, eats he probably eats his own hair."

My father wasn't impressed with my mother's doctor either. His trust had always been difficult to gain. He was raised on the west side of Detroit, less than a mile from the abandoned shell of Tiger Stadium in Cork Town, a borough originally settled by Irish immigrants and second-generation families of Northern European descent. During my father's youth, old men with leathery skin sold lake trout caught

46

from the Detroit River and pints of home-brewed stout from wood carts freighted with blocks of ice. Mothers and daughters grew potatoes the size of cantaloupes in the rich, dark soil of front yard gardens each summer. Fathers, sons and grandfathers pitched horseshoes in empty lots following their shifts at the Lynch Road assembly plant.

"Don't know if I can trust that doctor," he lamented on the way home from the hospital the night before my mother's release, referring to the doctor's ethnicity, which I found undeterminable. As a teenager, my father had been mugged by a group men who'd taken residence in an abandoned brownstone two blocks from his house as he trudged home from school one day. They often lounged on the weed-infested front stoop of the house after sundown, drinking quarts of Schlitz malt liquor and urinating in the overgrown baseball lot next door. My father had sustained two broken ribs and a cracked fingernail before giving up the two dollars in quarters he'd stuffed in his sweat sock to help defer the expense of his family's laundry bill each month. Sometimes, when he recalled the story to my sisters and me, he unconsciously touched his ribs and let out an exhausted sigh.

I looked up at the rear view mirror. Silver light from passing cars drifted across my father's rutted face as we drove, illuminating the gray half moons of skin that had begun to sag beneath his eyes since her admission. As I gazed into the mirror at his tired face, I began to think of all the trips we took in his car. Unlike my mother, my father enjoyed driving and found the low drone of tires against pavement soothing to his life consumed by us, work and mom's sickness. Once, maybe two months before she got sick, we drove through the forests and hills of the Upper Peninsula on our way to a campground late at night and I sat in front between them while Mom slept. For half an hour I listened to the hiss of air through my sisters' noses as they lay passed out in back. Janis Joplin whispered words to a song on the radio I could barely hear. I leaned toward my father, cupped my hand around his ear and whispered, "Punch it!"

"Shhh," he hissed, shooting a glance at my mother, who slept in the passenger seat with her head pushed up against the headrest. "Not so loud—wait a few more miles."

I nodded, then turned to look out the window. I could see the chiseled layers of orange, gray and brown rock and dusty sediment that had taken hundreds of years to form into the precise sequence of crust as our headlights flooded the roadside, impressed with the geographical accumulation of history that marked this part of the state. Land like this had never existed in the woods and around the lakes in the town where I grew up, which sat in a small valley some thirty miles west of Detroit. I peered at my father, his face lit by the green glow of the speedometer. He shot me a glance and winked. He was an experienced travel strategist and I trusted his judgement completely. To avoid waking my sisters and mother on these trips, he often let our 1969 Charger coast over rough spots in the road or else he carefully swerved the car to the soft shoulder to avoid potholes. Once, he pulled over late at night, twisted a half piece of tissue into a thin spiral and delicately threaded it into mom's ear to muffle the engine's drone. Then we sped off in a flurry of chewed up rock and gravel. But within four miles mom woke up, her petite body sensing the increase in velocity at which our car moved. She stared at my father, her eyes narrowed to slits.

His head shifted nervously between the road and Mom. "What?" he asked.

She patted her nest of blond hair, scrunching it back into place. "You know what," she said in an even voice, the twist of tissue sticking out of her ear. "Back it down."

She plucked the tissue from her ear, her squint still fixed on my father who stared straight ahead as the car slowed to a lower speed.

But now as we drove home from the hospital, his concern for her health and the ability of her doctor to make the right diagnoses distracted him. We'd already gone on a trip, but still mom got sick. After a few minutes, my father fidgeted in his seat, yawned, then shook his head a few times, as if trying to prevent himself from further comment regarding a strange doctor's potential for an incorrect diagnosis.

My sisters and I didn't know what to think. We were still disoriented by the suddenness with which her heart had seized up like a car engine that lacked enough oil. During visiting hours, we sat quietly beside Mom's bed, studying the clear plastic tubes plugged into her arms, through which transparent liquids flowed from the IV bag. On occasion she awoke and peered at us with a blank, inconsolable stare we'd never seen before, one that seemed to question who we were and what had happened as her vacant eyes roamed the room's perimeter. A glass vase filled with long stem roses, daisies and baby's breath sat on the window-side table where my sisters attempted to arrange the remaining components of Mom's makeup bag on our first visit: an aluminum tin of pink rouge placed at the center of the tabletop, fenced in by silver tubes of red, orange and mauve lipstick.

The scent of rubbing alcohol and sweat consumed the air, a combination that made my nose twinge and my eyes water each time I inhaled. Bolted to the wall opposite her bed sat a short row of blue plastic chairs with straight and uncomfortable backs. Above them hummed a 20-inch Zenith black and white television, attached by two metallic support beams that extended from the ceiling like silver arms holding out a gift. Everything—the flat, clinical musings of the doctor, the exhausted expressions on the faces of my father and sisters, the sterile environment in which she suffered, the sense of weightlessness I felt while standing next to Mom's bed, listening to the electronic bleat of the heart monitor on the stand beside her—felt staged, as if I observed the room from behind a plate glass window.

She suffered from a congenital heart condition characterized by an untraceable and sudden increase in the heart's rhythm, brought on by moments of intense nervousness or anxiety. The doctor speculated that a portion of her heart had ceased to function properly and finally suffered from a momentary delay in pumping, which caused the attack. Based on his estimate, eighty-percent of her mental faculties were expected to return, representing a substantial recovery given the deficit of oxygen her brain and heart had endured.

But our doubts regarding his prognosis grew following her homecoming. Words with precise, unwavering meanings gained new relevance when delivered from Mom's lipstick-painted mouth. The word look became gook; blew had transgressed into spew; car was now lard, an exchange that invoked chuckles from my sisters and I when Mom and Dad weren't looking. She'd even forgotten my name. A hospital psychiatrist informed us that this was something we should expect.

Still, the contrasts between who she was and who she'd become were sudden and unsettling in spite of the biological explanations and linguistic consequences. Before her illness, she'd attained a level of artistry in the use of swear words unparalleled by other mothers in our neighborhood, even those with large and untenable families who lived at the end of our street. Growing up, I often believed she was the author of many unchristian phrases. Her skill in verbally manipulating the behavior of my sisters and I was as equally daunting as her physical ability in restraining us with a tight squeeze of her hand on the fleshy part of our upper arms whenever we acted up in public. She was a small, delicate-looking woman prone to moments of controlled fierceness, and we avoided confrontation with her at all times. Out of habit, we'd adhered to this policy well into her first stay at home, when it was clear that her mind and memory had diminished beyond repair.

"Am I like before? What I was?" she asked me at the dinner table a year after her return. I didn't know how to respond. The five of us sat silent a few moments, surprised at her ability to make this abrupt, unexpected assessment, our heads bowed as we gazed at our watery mashed potatoes and blood-red roast beef that she'd spent four hours preparing. I wanted to remind her of my real name then, but I quickly realized that this was not the right time.

"You're more like it every day," Dad declared, recognizing my consternation in having to supply an answer. I watched his wide, hairy hand hover toward the center of the table to stir the potatoes. A thick layer of milky water had bubbled to the surface. Using the tip of his butter knife, he gently carved a canal from one edge of the potatoes to the center and watched as the soft, lumpy pile absorbed the liquid, clearly intrigued by the saturation process taking place before his eyes. Then he smiled and traced her hand with his pinky. "Good meal, hon."

But her speech and memory didn't improve. One afternoon almost two years after her initial ailment, Mom withdrew a cigarette from the pack she kept tucked in the breast pocket of her blue painting robe as we sat in the family room watching a Clint Eastwood movie. Then she carefully leaned forward, extended her hand and reached for her lighter that rested on the coffee table in front of the couch. But her trembling fingers accidentally knocked it to the floor.

She sat back and sighed, suddenly exhausted from expending what little energy she had, her cigarette still nestled between the index and middle fingers of her left hand. She pointed the butt end at the lighter. "Ann," she whispered, "pick that damn thing up and put it on the fuckis."

I turned around, glanced at her, then returned to watching television, caught off guard by this new word, particularly since it was the first time she incorrectly used a swear word in everyday conversation.

"What'd you say, Mom?" Sara asked. She sat Indian-style beside Mom on our black leather couch, her blond bangs concealing her eyes.

"The fuckis," she whispered again. "Put that on the fuckis."

Sara flicked her hair out of the way and squinted at her. "You mean the table?"

"Yes, yes," Mom repeated. She jabbed her cigarette at the table, then at the lighter once more as her frustration began to grow. "Put it on there. I need it."

"You heard her," Ann said, clenching her chin with a hand to restrain the smile that crept across her thin red lips. "Put it on the fuckis."

I sat on the floor with my back against the couch next to Sara's feet. "What's a fuckis?" I'd asked, trying to sound sincere.

Sara jabbed me between my ribs with her big toe, sending a rift of pain through my side.

"Adam, you didn't hear that," she hissed. "Don't let Dad hear you say that. He'll kick your scrawny ass." She jabbed me once more for emphasis.

"Would someone please put my Bic on the fuckis?" Mom asked again, oblivious to our conversation. I turned to look at her. A blue vein pulsed at the corner of her left eye, a physical imperfection I'd never seen before. I stretched a foot across the red carpet of our family room, squeezed the lighter between my toes, then brought it forward and tossed it over my shoulder back onto the coffee table, where it skittered across the top and nearly fell off the other side.

"Thank you, Kevin," Mom said. I started to turn toward her, but caught the glare of Sara's dark brown eyes and thought better of it.

Sara gently touched Mom's arm. "You mean Adam, right mom?" she asked, the nail of her big toe grazing my ribs.

Mom nodded. She plugged the cigarette into her mouth, lit it, and sucked until the ember glowed and smoke uncurled in front of her face. "Kevin, go find me an ashtray."

Sara reached for my hand as I stood up, but I took a step away from her. "Adam," she whispered as I turned toward the kitchen.

Fuckis, I murmured, trying to remind myself to write this new word down in the notebook I'd kept since my mother's return. At one time I believed the collection of her words might some day help identify the differences between this new version of who she'd become compared to who she once was. But no matter how hard I studied the different words and their disjointed spellings, I could never account for the changes that resulted from her illness.

I slunk toward the sink, where I used a steak knife to chisel out the butts that had been glued to the plastic ashtray by some noxious yellow substance, my head heavy with the uncertainty of who she believed I was. Kevin isn't such a bad name, I tried to convince myself as I rubbed my mother's ashtray, waiting for the fuzzy reflection of my face to appear on the dark plastic surface.

II

The Rifle

Alberts' father taught him how to shoot. Thirty-odd sixes, Browning Hi-Powers, a Marlin lever-action .22. This last rifle had always been his favorite. For the past ninety-years it had remained in his family, passed down to generations of blank-faced uncles and thin-eyed cousins he remembered from photographs stored in the dust-covered trunks of his father's attic: quiet, stubborn men who'd farmed the hazy flood plain of the Saginaw River without rest or imagination.

Alberts wasn't concerned with the route of ownership the rifle had taken, one which eventually led to him. When considered at length, it wasn't difficult to approximate the number of men in his family whose callused and mud-smeared hands once steadied the rifle against their shoulders: ten, maybe eleven. A small, immeasurable figure, but one that lent the weapon a historical texture his great aunts and uncles were unable to achieve during their brief and unremarkable lives. His recollections of who they were and how they lived, what part of Genesee County they were born into and the method by which they'd passed, had begun to subside by his fourteenth birthday. A few stories remained intact: tales of how they tended the clay-choked land with dull-teethed plows and rust-feathered hoes scavenged from abandoned farms that littered Saginaw County; or how they gently tugged out the bulbs of young vegetables in the impenetrable September heat, and filled the remaining holes with dirt and seed that yielded nothing but indignation the following season. Sometimes, as Alberts peered into his palms or pressed them to his mouth to warm and smell them on a November night, he wondered what percentage of his nubbed skin was composed by the complex webbing of ancestral tissue.

In most instances his family's use of the .22 was restricted to the close-range extermination of foxes, coyotes, and other animals that chewed holes in wire fences, killed chickens and pilfered vegetable gardens each month. Sometimes the weapon served other purposes. Once, Alberts heard a story described by a great aunt at a family reunion when he was a boy, an account of the drunken, unkempt life of Lem Rickson, a philosophizing, antagonizing, woman-izing, whiskey-pounding great uncle who'd tripped on a fallen tree trunk and accidentally shot himself in the gut with the rifle on a hunting trip north of Salmon Trout River during the twenties. "Drunk as a skunk, like always. Bled to death somewheres along the shore," she'd lamented, a frost-ed mug of Budweiser cradled delicately in her pudgy hands. But Alberts hadn't taken the time to investigate this murky and unsubstantiated detail of his history. By 1921 the balance of his family had given up on their land and moved south to Flint or Pontiac to work in the automobile plants that had sprouted like barbed weeds along the edge of vacant pastures and the green, temperate meadows north of the county line.

He inherited the rifle from his father. The stock, constructed of hand-carved walnut, contained several scratches and dents that had been filled haphazardly with wood putty over the years. At one point during the gun's existence, someone had refinished the wood with an inadequate, oil-based varnish, one that had spawned blemishes along the length of stock like a parasitic wood disease. Three of the letters from the manufacturer's name inscribed on the barrel had been worn smooth by the tensed fingers of family members, but the action remained fluid and precise. A good weapon—compact, sturdy, simple to control and manipulate.

That's how his father characterized the rifle. During weekends up north, Alberts learned the mechanics and respect indispensable to the Marlin's use as he trudged through his father's one-hundred and twenty acres, searching for squirrels that traversed the oak limbs stretched above him, or rustled invisibly in the leaf-infested ravines carved throughout the property. None of his excursions made any sense: whenever he saw a rabbit or a squirrel—hunched on its hind legs in front of him, clinging precariously to the trunk of a birch, or resting along the rock-studded shore of the Green River, chewing furiously on a nut or berry—the joints in his fingers locked up and his vision grew dark, making it impossible to aim and squeeze off a round. Some days he didn't even attempt to raise the gun to his shoulder: by fourteen he'd realized that he hadn't the coolness of emotion or the stomach required of hunters. Most times he simply ended his search for squirrels or rabbits and expended his father's ammunition on tree trunks, upended stumps, telephone polls, and hand-carved signs that announced the local presence of the DNR hidden somewhere among the leafy growth of ferns and poplars.

"You need to be more aware of your surroundings," his father explained one late Saturday afternoon at the cabin. "Learn to conceal your smell; step lightly."

The two of them sat outside on the wood deck, watching the shadows from tall oaks and Austrian Pines stretch across the grassy meadow below. "Sometimes I forget things," Alberts admitted over the drone of crickets. "I can't always remember what to do."

"No?"

Alberts frowned. "Sometimes, but not always."

His father puffed air into his stubbled cheeks, which ballooned a moment before deflating, a response Alberts was unfamiliar with. "It's an equitable skill. When I was young, your grandfather and I used to come up here and take a few deer each season. The meat would last all winter and spring."

"I don't mind the quietness, or walking around the woods," Alberts conceded. "I like to shoot."

"But no killing," his father said, squinting into the meadow.

Alberts nodded.

"That's part of it: getting outside, having the opportunity to clear your head." He paused a moment. "Some day you might have a change of mind."

He stood up. With some lethargy he placed his hands on the small of his back and stretched. Inside his rib cage a few bones clicked and snapped. He arched his back again, swung his head from side to side, then turned and glided through the front room of the cabin, across the faded brown pelt of a medium-sized black bear he'd shot three seasons ago, and into the wood-paneled kitchen. In the far corner leaned the Remington 30-30 and Marlin. Alberts turned, listening to his father raise the .22 to his hip. He disengaged the lever, rotated the rifle on its side and quickly examined the receiver. Once his inspection was completed, he turned and walked back to the front porch, the Marlin cradled in his arms. He held the rifle before him and Alberts as if displaying a particularly large fish.

"This is a good weapon." He raised it up and down, studying the glint of light from the overcast day as it moved along the stock and barrel. "Learned to hunt with it. Ammunition's costly enough. I'd prefer if it wasn't wasted on trees and outhouses."

Alberts felt his face turn red. His father shouldered the rifle, squeezed it against his deltoid, and took aim down into the meadow. "I've seen you a few times," he said, moving his head up and down to find a comfortable position, the meat of his cheek flopping against the rifle stock. "Sometimes when you walk back along the northern edge of the fire road, just before you enter the meadow. From the bathroom window, you can look straight down the tree line, up that little rise before it takes you over the ridge. You like that old, dried-out husk of a stump, the one with those gray roots that look like plumbing. I believe that's what you're shooting at." He angled his opened eye at Alberts, the gun still leveled at the meadow. "Am I right?"

"I guess," Alberts said, uncertain of his father's accuracy. "If I do, I don't do it a lot. Just when I get bored and haven't seen anything for a while. Sometimes I don't even know I'm doing it."

"I figured that maybe you'd cornered a squirrel or rabbit," his father said, refocusing his aim. Alberts shook his head.

"Well. Anyway," his father murmured. He spread his legs apart and lowered the gun from his cheek. "Just keep it to a minimum. Otherwise you'll have to start buying those cheap shells."

He repositioned the rifle and again took aim. "Almost a hundred years old. Weight is still the same," he whispered, the gun pressed hard against his shoulder. "Sight still perfect."

He took some heavy breaths. Alberts listened to the whistle of air through his father's hairy nose. "See that short Jack Pine down there, the one just to the left of that small stand of birches? In line with the cabin."

Alberts peered into the meadow, his eyes moving along the clumps of wiry sagebrush, past the thin white birch trees until he located the pine. "I see it."

"Keep your eye on it. Tell me if it moves."

He aimed for several seconds, one eye pinched shut. Alberts lowered his face into his hands, gazed into the meadow as instructed and observed the jack pine for movement. His father squeezed the trigger and fired a shot. A few sparrows, flitting in the nearby trees, suddenly launched themselves into the air and circled chaotically in front of the porch before disappearing into the woods behind the cabin.

A thread of gun smoke hovered between Alberts and his father. Alberts cupped his hands around his eyes and studied the Jack Pine, which stood still in the pink and gray half-light that now consumed the meadow. In the distance, the gunshot echoed over the trees, into valleys and along the smooth surface of the Green River, then slowly faded. "I don't think you hit it," he said, peering through the smoke at his father.

"Don't think I even came close." He gazed at the grassy hump of earth upon which the Jack Pine stood, then turned to address Alberts. "Give it a shot," he said, handing Alberts the rifle. "We're a good two hundred yards out, but you never know."

"That's alright."

"Just try it. Maybe young eyes can see it more clearly than me."

Alberts shook his head and tentatively took the gun from his father's outstretched hand. He pressed the rifle against his bony shoulder, counted to three, then held his breath and took aim at the small tree. He squeezed the trigger and listened to the explosion of gunpowder ring in his ears.

"I missed," he said, lifting his chin from the rifle to observe the pine through the cloud of gun smoke. He stood back, then set the gun against the railing.

Alberts looked up at his father. The skin beneath his father's left eye twitched and his lower lip fluttered. "You get the point," he said. "This is a good weapon. Don't abuse it."

He turned back to his chair and settled into it. "Do you still like venison?" he asked, his voice high, tentative. "If I keep making those steaks, will you still eat them? I'd hate to see them go to waste."

Alberts looked into the meadow, contemplating the frailty of the Jack Pine, thankful for the growing inaccuracy of both his and his father's aim. "I still like it," he said.

His father nodded, then scanned the bend of trees that rimmed the meadow, envisioning venison steaks and jerky aging in the musty, web-infested outhouse that now served as the smoke room out back. Alberts watched his father's eyes. Some days he wasn't sure what he saw when he slumped into his chair, a sweating glass of bourbon and ginger ale squeezed between his thighs, and peered into the meadow. Maybe the tilt of grass from a fox, or the flash of a cardinal as it darted between the gnarled trunks of elm trees. Whenever his gaze traveled the weedy edge of the woods or followed the smooth fire road into the forest, a set of lines emerged at the corner of his sockets and the bones in his jaw grew hard. A look of concentrated, evenly controlled anger. Alberts had witnessed it many times: in lines at the bank on Saturday mornings; at the shop during long weekends as the grease-smeared machinists worked relentlessly to complete a job, their bald heads dimpled with sweat beneath the recessed light of fluorescent bulbs; at night watching women parade back and forth in their bikinis on the Playboy Channel, the glow of the television casting shadows in the hollows of his father's sockets.

He turned and reviewed Alberts with an expression he often wore when inspecting a die that had sustained a hairline crack: large brown eyes opened wide, the tip of his tongue pressed to his upper lip. "Maybe a few years from now you'll appreciate it more," he said, his tongue finally retreated into the blackness of his mouth. "Maybe you can humor me and go out sometime next year."

They sat a moment without speaking. A gust of wind moved through, stirring the upper branches of the trees, carrying the scent of pine.

"Maybe," Alberts murmured, though he'd longed sensed his desire to hunt diminishing months before. "If I could do it without actually having to kill, I'd probably be better at it."

His father stared into the meadow and shook his head in bewilderment. "Can't hunt without killing," he chuckled, though to Alberts it had the effect of a cackle. He took a sip from his glass; two rivulets of bourbon and ginger ale dribbled down his chin and onto his chest. "At least you like to get out and shoot," he said, dabbing at the wet spots with his index finger. "Don't ever stop doing that."

Weather Patterns

My brother and I ran together during breaks from college. Four miles was the average length of our run. This was subject to change, depending on the weather conditions and my level of energy. On most occasions, I had a difficult time keeping up with Justin. He'd been an All-American cross-country runner in high school and college, and he'd continued with the sport well into his graduate school years, competing in half marathons in towns near Detroit and along the borders of Indiana and Ohio. The run was always most important to him. Growing up, he believed it relieved his allergies to pollen, dust and mold, and reduced the potential of his epilepsy flaring up—biological theories he hadn't the means or desire to prove. Most times when we were home from college, we jogged four, five, even six miles if we took the long way through town past the paper mill.

One day during a Thanksgiving weekend we stopped at Piper's Point to rest, talk, and smoke a joint. It took several minutes for us to negotiate the path that lead to the Point: throughout my childhood and teenage years it was consistently gorged by seasonal rains, which made our hikes to the cliff edge arduous and cumbersome treks. Once we'd reached the top, I stood a moment and gazed down at the dark water that had surrounded me my entire life. Miles out into Lake Superior the horizon turned into a seamless hue of white mist and blue water that stretched beyond the western flap of land that marked the far end of the Upper Peninsula. Near the edge of the bluff sat a pile of charred stones that had been thrown together into a circle many years earlier to create a burning pit. Justin and I scouted around the rim of the forest, located some kindling, and then started a fire.

An old wooden milk crate sat beside the pit, stuffed with a tattered brown comforter. He reached in and removed the comforter, spread it on the cool ground so we could sit, then dug inside his sweat sock. His thick fingers bulged against the fabric until he withdrew a small joint flattened into a sheath of paper. He fingered the joint for several seconds, squeezing it into shape.

"Nice," I said, watching him cup a hand around the joint and ignite it with a burning twig. "How are we gonna hit that?"

He raised his eyebrows. "Smoked pinners worse than this," he declared, taking several quick draws until the ember glowed and smoke uncurled from between his teeth. He handed the joint to me.

For a while we sat and puffed. With my eyes I followed the wisps of smoke rising from the store chimneys in town and contemplated the hazy outline of the surrounding forest and hills. I stared out at the water, past the rusty buoys whose foggy red beacons blinked every three seconds. Half a mile out an oil tanker slid past. The wind turned and the odor of the Ottawan Grill drifted upwards—a concoction of tomatoes, stale beer and mustard that mixed with the smell of burning wood from our fire.

"That smell," I murmured, "reminds me of sweaty gym socks. Especially in the summer when it's really hot."

Justin took a breath, considering the scent.

"By the way," he said after a moment, "I'm going to Indiana and Kansas with a research group from school once classes are finished. We're helping a professor do some field research on tornadoes."

"Tornadoes?" I asked and glanced at the doobie; the oily resin had seeped out the end and smudged my fingertip. I licked the resin clean, took a hit and held the smoke in my lungs a few seconds.

"Take measurements, track and videotape them," he explained as I exhaled. "Like that t.v. show. What's it called, Video Reporter, Video Journalist? Video something, with all those weather guys who chase tornadoes."

"Something like that," I said, surprised at his plans.

He turned and squinted at me distrustfully. "You're the only one I've told so far," he said, "so don't say anything to Mom and Dad."

I nodded, acknowledging the reason for his reluctance in telling me this: as a boy I sometimes lost my head under our parents' scrutiny when they had reason to believe we were keeping things from them, or had conducted ourselves inappropriately while they were away for the day. "It's just a possibility," Justin explained.

I stared back at the bay, beyond the brown field grass along the lip of the bluff. As I watched the water, my eyes gre heavy with each wave that curled and tucked itself into the rocky beach, then unfolded as the undertow flowed outward. I placed the joint on a rock near my foot and picked up a wet string of grass from the ground. I turned back to Justin and flung it at him. The blade landed on his head, perfectly intersecting the border where his blond hair and forehead met. I laughed and flexed my shoulder beneath my sweat-soaked t-shirt, preparing for the swift thud of his fist against it. He put his hand up and I winced in anticipation. But instead of punching me he simply peeled the blade of grass from his skin and glared at me.

"Ass," he hissed, his lips fluttering into a smile. "Quit fucking around and listen to me. I figure it'll be good to get some field experience. Get out of the class a while, learn a few things. What do you think?"

"Me?" I asked. I shook my head at the image of him and a group of students packed shoulder-to-shoulder in a two-door compact car, attempting to manage their bulky equipment as they tracked a tornado, completely oblivious to its shifting path. "Why not. Might be fun."

He leaned forward and motioned his head towards the joint. "Hand me the fatty," he said. I passed it to him, finger to finger.

"And Mom and Dad don't know yet?"

"No," he sputtered, holding his breath, the joint now pinched between his thumb and forefinger. "Waiting for the right time. Maybe I'll say something before I go back Sunday."

"Can you wait until I'm out of the house for the day," I asked him.

Justin handed the joint to me and began fiddling with a small black twig near his foot. "I will," he said, fully aware of the reaction our father might have to the news. Justin squinted at me, then peered at the ground a few seconds without speaking. "Actually, I've been thinking about staying at school a while and finding a job," he said. "Take a semester or two off and get a few things straight in my head. Make a little money."

"Really?" I said, surprised at his desire to live in troll territory below the Mackinaw Bridge.

"I think so. Might be good to scratch out a living for a while."

We smoked a while longer without speaking. Finally he said, "My timing's not the greatest. This morning Mom asked me how I was doing and when I might finish. Told her maybe next year, depending on how classes go. If I go back."

We sat a while longer staring down at the town, watching cars pass dribble through. I considered what he said, but couldn't understand why my parents were suddenly concerned about him completing his studies. Whenever his grades arrived in December or in early May from his university in Detroit, my father would trot down the gravel driveway, throw open the plastic mailbox door, then hustle back to the house, the loose flesh around his chest jiggling underneath his t-shirt. He would gather my mother and I around the kitchen table and slice the blue envelope open with a butter knife, his fingers trembling as if he'd expected this to be notification that he'd won the Publisher's Sweepstakes. Finally he'd squint a few moments at the carbon copy of Justin's report card, nod, then plop it down on the table for us to review.

Justin never saw my father perform this little exhibition: most times he was at school, preparing for the next semester, or on his way home for a visit. Had he been home to witness this performance, I secretly believed that he wouldn't have taken any part in my father's drama. My brother realized at an early age that he and I were different, and as we grew older the differences became more clearly defined. He was a better, more balanced athlete, more proficient at board and card games, more patient when learning new things. I wasn't a very good student. During holiday breaks, following the arrival of my grades from the small community college that I attended in Iron Mountain, I sat at the kitchen table and suffered through my father's litany concerning the importance of education. After two fruitless semesters I learned to identify what grades he was reviewing by closely observing the physical movements of his body: a hand tucked deep into the back pocket of his grease-stained jeans, or an awkward, rocking motion of his thick body as he stood in front of me, indicated his uncertainty at mentioning the C's I'd received in trigonometry and biology. These marks I regarded as unexpected gifts.

Some day, I often thought to myself as I sat before my father, my gaze fixed upon the delicate yellow flowers of our kitchen table cloth, I might walk behind my son as he sat hunched over the kitchen table, trying to decipher the reasons he failed to perform well in school.

"You wanna screw off, fine—use your own goddamn money!" my father's voice often boomed.

"Alan, your language," my mother would interrupt from across the table where the two of us sat.

My father would continue, ignoring my mother. "Better yet, I'd like to see you get a scholarship like your brother. Then you'll see how important it is!"

Justin hadn't actually received a scholarship—more precisely, a four year fellowship to study meteorology at Wayne State University in Detroit. But I never mentioned this difference to my father.

"Okay, okay, I'm sorry," I would blurt. "I'll do good next semester."

"Well—well!" my mother would shout in correction, her voice cracking as she anxiously wrung her hands together and glared from across the table at me. "You will do *well.*"

"Goddamn it," my father would bark. Most times his voice was so loud the carbon copy of my report card quivered as it rested in the middle of the oak table. Then, after regaining his composure, he'd sit next to my mother, cup his big leathery hands together on the table, lean forward and say, "Darrel, you gotta stop goofing off now. You're older. We can't afford to pay for this ... this shit any more. You've got to make a stronger attempt. Put more commitment into it. My God, you're what.....21 now? Don't you think it's time?"

"We pay good money for you to attend that school, Darrel," my mother would add. "The only benefit it seems to have given you is more opportunity to run around during the day and do God knows what at night. Is that how you want to live your life? Dink around, do nothing all day? Your brother understands what he needs to do to be successful in this life."

"I don't know," I would mutter, sincerely at a lost for words or reasons.

"You don't know?" My father would sneer, shooting a blank stare at my mother. "He doesn't know? What the hell does that mean?"

The words were always the same. Screw off. Own money. Scholarship. My father would motion to my mother and say, "We are retiring in a few years. One day the mill will close. We're not young anymore. Look at your mother. See the lines? The gray hairs? That's from worrying about you. We can't retire until you get your butt in gear. Understand!"

I would hang my head, feigning dissatisfaction with my grades as well. After a moment of silence, I would look at the both of them and say, "I understand. I'll do good next semester."

Then my mother would slowly close her eyes. "Well," she'd lament, shaking her head. "The proper word is Well."

I glanced over at Justin sitting next to me on the bluff. Around us, the trees were already naked that Thanksgiving: dead, wet leaves carpeted the forest floor. A twig was threaded between the fingers of his right hand, and he began bending it into a half circle. I watched, curious at the flexibility his fingers were able to work into that moist, damp twig as he slowly molded the limb into an oval. It didn't snap. With my thick, stubby fingers, the branch would never have stood a chance—no sense of touch like Justin. Like everything else, I learned to accept and appreciate the differences between us.

Justin cleared his throat and looked down at the twig. "Don't say anything to Mom and Dad," he said, "but I really don't think I'm going back to school for my last year. At least not right now."

"What?" I asked. "Not at all?"

"I'd like to make a little money," he said solemnly. "Pay off some of my credit cards. I've racked them up pretty high."

We didn't speak for a moment or two.

"You sure about this?" I finally asked. "Only a year left."

Justin stared at the town. A crow flew over the bay, then turned south and circled above our bluff.

"I don't know," he sighed, staring up at the bird as it cawed against the white sky and vanished over the forest behind us. "Doesn't feel the same anymore. I've lost interest."

He paused, made a small clicking noise inside his mouth, and grinned. "Know how long it's been since I've been with a girl?" he asked.

"A girl?"

"Take a guess."

I studied a series of wrinkles that had sprouted at the corner of his right eye since the last time I saw him. "I don't know—three, four months," I guessed. "Maybe five."

He shook his head. "Almost eight."

"Eight?" I chuckled. "Eight months?" I said again, genuinely shocked. "That's a record."

He raised his hands up and shrugged. "A girl from one of my lectures," he said. "I don't have any time for anything else. Sleep, eat and study, that's it. That's been my life."

"Eight months," I cackled, still amazed.

"Alright, don't make a big deal about it."

"Have you considered coming back up here?" I asked, though I knew his answer to this question.

He shook his head and smiled faintly. "I'll still be back for holidays and visits."

I chewed the inside of my lip a minute. "I guess you're lucky," I whispered. "With your education I bet you'll find something pretty quick."

He nodded. After a moment he stood up and walked to the edge of the bluff to consider the small line of cars that had stopped at the light of Main Street and Fountain below us. People craned their heads out of their windows and gazed up at the sky, watching the white smoke float upward from our fire. Sheriff Perkins' mud-smeared blazer pulled up beside the drug store, and then his gray head slowly emerged from the driver's window. Sunlight broke through the clouds and glinted sharply off his aviator sunglasses. With his paint-flecked bullhorn in his hand, he garbled a few words of warning up at us.

"The Perk is acting up," Justin said, offering Sheriff Perkins a large, swooping wave. The sheriff shook his head, then ground the truck through its gears until the vehicle disappeared down the street.

We sat on the bluff a while longer without speaking and smoked the joint, then started in on the seven roaches that Justin had saved in a zip-lock freezer bag for later that weekend. He dug into his sock, stopped, scratched his ankle, peered at the coils of brown hair on his skin, then removed the bag with two fingers. He reminded me of a detective handling evidence in a movie or t.v. show—his mouth cut into a straight, unmoving line across his face, eyes clenched in concentration, his movements slow and deliberate.

"Come on, come on, let's go!" I whined. "Pull them out!"

I shot a hand towards the bag, but he anticipated my move and swung around so that his back blocked my attempt.

"Hurry up," I hissed and settled back.

Finally we smoked and in less than an hour the roaches were gone. Our fire had died out and we huddled close to the glowing embers, waiting for the buzz to catch up. When it had, we stood and stumbled towards the edge of the bluff and gazed down at the town. A few cars passed on Main Street, followed again by Sheriff Perkins' truck. Inside the cab we could see his head shift from side to side as he examined the storefronts. A wisp of smoke trickled from our fire, but the sheriff hadn't noticed. More cars passed. A minute later our father's Buick came lumbering through, the car's rattling, rust-eaten pipe popping between the brick buildings and the limestone cliffs.

"Jesus," Justin muttered from the corner of his mouth, "you can hear that crappy thing all the way up here. Why can't he just fix it."

My father gunned the car engine. I turned to Justin, who winced as the tail pipe gurgled below us. I smiled, shook my head and stared down at my father, his face now aimed toward our bluff. For a moment he seemed to watch something in the sky behind us, perhaps a crow or hawk circling above the dense, leafless forest. I observed him a few more seconds; he smiled and gave us a small wave.

Amazing, I thought to myself: the resemblance between him and Justin was clearly recognizable, even from the bluff. I saw Justin's face reflected in my father's deep eye sockets, square jaw and small pug nose. The web of squint lines at the corners of my fathers' eyes wasn't visible from this distance, but I knew it was there.

Justin and I stood next to each other, silently watching our father.

"I can't believe how much you look like him," I whispered.

My brother dropped his hand. "I know," he said. "Don't remind me."

Justin and I had our last run together the following spring. It was a cool, overcast May day: white bursts of apple blossoms brushed the tips of branches along the roads, shore banks and hills that rose above Munson Bay. The last hunks of winter ice began their drift past the limestone formations that jutted into the mouth of the bay like knobby fingers. We were racing the last mile of our run for a quart of Mickey's beer. Justin was ahead. He glanced over his shoulder at me and began to slow down.

"Come on," he shouted, his head bobbing up and down in time with the sound of his Nikes slapping the earth. "If you wanna catch me you gotta run faster."

"Just keep running," I yelled back.

Then his pace slowed considerably. As usual, I assumed he was offering me the opportunity to beat him. I reduced my pace as well. After a few more feet, he stopped completely and bent over to catch his breath, his hands pressed against his knees, face red and streaked with sweat. I caught up, bent down next to him and asked, "What's up?"

He closed his eyes, shook his head, then traced the side of his face with a finger. "I think I'm getting a headache," he heaved. "My face feels numb. I gotta rest."

We stood up. Behind him, patches of the lake were visible through the trees. A rusty fish trawler chugged by, dangerously close to the shore, the top half of its gray fish net barely visible on the surface of the lake. Justin placed his hands on his back and took a deep breath. He peered up at the sky through the web of tree branches and said, "Jesus, Darryl, my head hurts."

He looked back down and held a hand out in front of us. Suddenly each finger began to twitch uncontrollably, as if regulated by its own electrical impulse. The trembling traveled into his hand, up his arm, and crossed over into his neck, causing his veins to bulge against his skin. "F-fuck," he wheezed. He searched my face, as if questioning the movement of his body, and reached toward my arm. I took it in my hand and cautiously led him to the dirt shoulder.

"Take it easy, Justin," I said, and then clenched his arm tighter, trying to figure out what to do. I couldn't remember the last time he had an epileptic seizure in front of me—a year, maybe two. But that didn't account for any he may have had at school.

The road was empty. Justin's trembling intensified, causing his teeth to chatter. I gazed through the trees for the boat on the water and watched the tail end of it move north away from the bay and out of sight.

I cupped my hands around my mouth. "Hey!" I shouted, but as soon as I did Justin staggered forward and collapsed into a ditch filled with water. His body convulsed. His hands and legs slapped and kicked the water, and his eyes had fluttered up into his head. I jumped in, clutched his shoulders and turned him over, then tightened my grip and attempted to force my fingers into his mouth. Saliva frothed on his lips and mixed with the blood from his bitten tongue. When I was young my parents told me that if he ever bad a seizure in front of me and I had nothing to hold his tongue with, pinch it so that it wouldn't slip down his throat.

"Pinch it," my father had instructed me years before, holding his knobby thumb and forefinger close to my face, "like a pair of pliers."

We kept a jar of tongue depressors in the house for such occurrences. As a boy, I often listened to him and our parents struggle in the bathroom during his seizures, dumping over glass shampoo bottles that rested on the edge of the tub, sending toothbrushes skittering across the counter and onto the tiled floor. By my eighth birthday, I had grown accustomed to the noise and frantic activity associated with his seizures. In most cases, they usually ended after twenty minutes.

I tried to clamp onto Justin's tongue but it slipped through my grip. Water poured into his mouth, bubbled out his nostrils and flowed into his eyes. At one point his teeth cut into my fingers, causing my blood to rush warm over my knuckles and his cheeks. After a few minutes his tongue escaped my grip and caught in his throat, immediately cutting off air flow. I thrust my fingers deep into his mouth, trying to retrieve his tongue, but I was unable to reach it. A second or two later Justin had stopped breathing, but I kept pushing my fingers into his mouth until I found his tongue.

For a long time I sat in the ditch with his head in my lap, wiping the blood from his lips and cheeks. I didn't feel the rain come down from Canada, a wet sheet that engulfed the town in a white mist. I could see the water of the lake sway and the rain drops dimple the surface. A few threads of lightning blinked across the sky above the trees, followed by the low rumble of thunder through the wet valleys and hills of Munson Bay. Mud swelled around our feet and legs, creating streams that gathered twigs and leaves into their current, then disappeared into the woods. I thought of all the places the rain water would carry our sweat and blood, the tiny crevices in the earth thousands of miles away, where twigs and leaves would eventually come to settle without anyone ever noticing.

The rain ended. Out in the darkness and fog I heard a truck grumble toward me and stop as its engine rattled into silence. Then I felt Sheriff Perkins lift and help me into the front seat of his truck. He sloshed back along the road side to Justin still heaped in the ditch where I had left him, his shorts and shirt plastered with mud. Sheriff Perkins didn't say anything to me once he got into the truck. On the way home I leaned my head against the window, stared out at the wet hills and forest as they passed, and listened to the vacant drone of the tires against the wet pavement.

"You really think I look like Dad?" Justin asked as we stood on the bluff and listened to our father's Buick burble through town. In the air lingered the smell of Thanksgiving turkey. We'd smoked all of our pot and it was time to go home for dinner.

"A bit. Same eyes and mouth." I looked around at his rear end, now covered with clumps of moist dirt. "Same ass."

"Hmm," he said. "That's not so bad." He put his hands to his mouth and blew, warming them. "You about ready?"

I nodded and stared at him, unsure what to say about his intentions to leave school and move down state and possibly out west and out of my life. Soon he would be gone and I would be left to jog around Munson Bay by myself on Sundays, past Guernt's restaurant, with its massive black-and-white aerial photograph of town dangling by reinforced fish line in the window. By then, it was easy to imagine myself alone, cooling down under the rusty awning of the Eight Ball pool hall, staring through the window. I would stand quietly and watch the men shoot pool, suck deeply on cigarettes and swig bottles of Budweiser under the battered light fixtures that swayed back and forth whenever the tip of a player's cue accidentally hit them. One day I would learn the names of each player: Gene Lyndy, a middle-aged, white -haired man who wore red and black flannel shirts every day of the year and made his living poaching deer in the land between our town and the foot of the Porcupine Mountains at the western end of the Upper Peninsula, an area of the forest the DNR couldn't adequately patrol; Bill James Wilkes, a mechanic whose bloated-looking hands were perpetually stained with oil and lubrication grease no matter how vigorously he scrubbed them at the deep sink of Jet's Auto Repair in town; and Everette Grosell, 91, former mayor of Munson Bay and sole proprietor of the pool hall, a man whose face was so rutted with wrinkles it was difficult to ascertain from a distance which crevices contained his light blue eyes. At times they might turn and acknowledge my presence with a nod, perhaps including me in their Sunday rituals, but eventually their gazes would lift from my body and focus on the stretch of water that lay without end across the street. Maybe that view was all they ever needed, I would wonder. I would watch them closely, my fingers pressed hard against the cool glass, and understand that destiny for some people in Munson Bay would always be connected to a tradition men like these had unknowingly forged by not leaving.

I turned back to Justin. He shook his head, as if suggesting to me not to say a word: his decision to leave school and Munson Bay altogether was firm. I nodded my agreement, then turned and started for the path. We moved cautiously down the hill and through the woods to the main road, the wet mud sucking at our shoes. A light rain had begun to fall. Once on the road, I raised my face to the sky and walked some twenty yards with my head in that position, feeling the water pelt my eyelids and lips, a sensation I'd enjoyed since I was a little boy.

Justin moved in closer to me. "Ya know," he whispered, his shoulder bumping against mine, "a bird could piss on you right now and you'd have no idea." He chuckled and quickened the pace of our walk. I opened my eyes and searched the sky above and in front of me for any birds that may have just passed over. Bare tree branches stretched towards the sky.

He was ahead of me and soon broke into a steady jog. I followed him through town, past Guernt's and back up Cider Mill Road, until we hit Junction Island Road, where we ran the washed-out shoulder beneath the leafless trees for two miles. "Last few yards for a beer," he yelled back at me, but by then I could see that he was already slowing down. We were a half a mile from our house.

I accelerated and caught up to him.

"Holy shit, Darrel," he gasped, forcing a smile. "You pick today to finally kick my ass?"

"Just run," I managed to say, surprised at myself but unsure if I could keep up the pace. He had always slowed for me in the past when I fell behind him, but now that we were even, I wanted him to run harder and faster.

He lurched forward and let out a muffled groan. Clenching my fists, I pumped my legs more swiftly and caught him again as our house, set against the forest wall on a hill that overlooked the dirt road and the valley below us, came into view. My mother, standing under the brown nylon awning of our front door, gestured to my father as he stepped from his car. He stood, a brown grocery bag tucked under one arm, and turned to watch our approach.

"You got me!" Justin laughed, but it wasn't true: we still remained even as we raced the last few yards to the front door of our house.

Holes

Evan discovered his grandmother's pistol, a nickel-plated .38 caliber revolver that smelled of gun oil, wedged in her bureau drawer beneath an envelope filled with four hundred dollars. A box of bullets, stuffed inside an old stocking streaked with runs, rested beside the gun. He reached in, took out the silky black bundle, then hooked a finger around the trigger guard and slowly removed the gun. He held it a few seconds, feeling the balance and weight of it in his palm, watching sunlight reflect off the nickel plating. He fingered the words Smith & Wesson engraved on the barrel and the phrase .38 caliber, tiny letters and numbers still filled with deposits of cleaning oil.

He spun the empty cylinder with his forefinger until all six cartridge cavities clicked, then pulled the hammer back and aimed out the bedroom window at a fat pigeon perched on a power line. The bird surveyed the garden, its small grey head shifting back and forth, then released a white splotch that dropped heavily to the ground below. His arm wavered, unaccustomed to the concentrated weight of the gun. But for the most part the revolver felt good in his hand. He glanced at the bird again as it picked and nuzzled its chest.

With his left eye focused, he held his breath a few seconds, squeezed the trigger, then winced as the hammer snapped harmlessly against the firing pin.

He lowered the weapon. With his forefinger, he traced the groves and chiseled steel of the barrel. A gun? he whispered. Using his pinky, he plugged the barrel, rotated the revolver and examined the cylinder for cartridges. Empty. Why a gun? But the answer to his question had been buried with her body three weeks ago. Attempts to clarify it, make it comprehensible, seemed useless and uninspired. Besides, he wasn't terribly surprised at how calmly he handled her loss. In many ways it seemed as distant and unreal as his grandfather Bubby's death when Evan was nine months old. But as he cleared out his grandmother's closets in the front room two weeks ago—folding her flowery dresses and polyester slacks, crushing old shoe boxes that held his preschool drawings of houses, forests and contorted animals, binding a box of decaying letters his grandfather had written during the first war from the muddy trenches of France—Evan discovered things about her he hadn't known existed before her death. He found notes taped in spots he planned on cleaning before selling the condo, little scribblings in red and blue ink that detailed what to do with her things once she was gone. One, taped to a space on the wall behind the clothes in her closet, read

Evan, see to it that Aunt Marion gets all my skirts and blouses, especially the more colorful ones. Many of them are new and it would be a waste not to have someone wear them. They just hang on me now with all the weight that I lost last month with the flu.

Evan turned and peered into the living room where sunlight now flooded through the balcony door onto the wood floor and stucco walls. Some items still remained in the kitchen, living room and bedroom where he had grown up—her dresser where he'd found the gun, a painting of the aqua ocean and Lake Michigan shoreline hanging above the TV, a leafy plant crawling up the corner from its frayed wicker pot. But now his grandmother's scent—a combination of Oil of Olay and Ben Gay—was gone, erased from the condo the same week he swept up the clouds of dust balls and scraps of paper that littered the floors.

He raised the gun and aimed at the area where the couch and end tables used to sit, then at the balcony where he placed a few garbage bags the other day. The small things that had decorated these spaces for the last forty years— pewter picture frames that contained yellowing photographs of her parents standing on the front steps of their home in East Detroit in the late teens; the pile of black-and-white coasters molded in the shape of Mickey Mouse's face; white porcelain ashtrays she'd bought at some garage sale—were gone. He'd cleaned them up, boxed them, and shipped them to the last of his grandmother's cousins in Texas and Arizona, distant relatives who failed to attend the funeral due to sickness or old age. Evan hadn't seen any of them for over twenty years. He found it a bit disheartening that they couldn't muster the strength to come and say their final good-byes. Once, when he was eight or nine, he'd met a few of them at some get together in a VFW hall on the west side of Detroit: gray-haired aunts who passed around foggy Polaroidsof their grandchildren, and balding uncles hunched at the bar, gulping pints of beer and mumbling about the days when they'd worked at the Lynch Road assembly plant before the war. Those aunts and uncles had become nothing more than distant voices who called at Thanksgiving and Christmas, people who often forgot Evan's age.

The larger things, like the huge Zenith Trinitron and a rosewood credenza upon which she had placed a photograph of him in his college hockey jersey, were sold in a lawn sale he'd orchestrated on the tiny strip of sun-dried grass in front of her building. He'd set up everything as it had looked in her condo: the purple suede couch seven feet in front of the television; the credenza to its right, propped against some chubby green bushes that looked to have sprouted from the building's cracked foundation; end tables at each end of the couch. Once all was in order, he stood on the sidewalk and framed the setting between his hands the way a movie director might crop a scene as traffic roared past and whipped his dark hair against his face.

He hefted the gun in his palm a few times. There wasn't a scratch on it, unlike the other things that had suffered dents and abrasions here and there during the move to the front lawn. Lugging her furniture down the metal staircase with only a few minutes of help from the superintendent had been a difficult chore, one that left Evan's body wracked with knots of pain. She would've understood if some things were damaged, he figured, rubbing a sore muscle on his back. He squeezed the gun in his hand and wished he could have kept a few items—the blue velvet footrest her Siamese cat Jezabell slept on when she was alive twelve years ago, a few wisps of fur still plastered to the fabric; the brown leather Lazy-Boy recliner, where she'd sit watching Lion games on Sundays, a mug of beer balanced delicately in her lap.

"Boys," she'd proclaim after each Lion turnover. "That's all they are. Little boys playing a man's game."

But there wasn't enough room in his apartment for what he wanted to keep. Instead, he'd sat in a lawn chair in front of the building, trying to decipher her financial papers and Social Security forms heaped in his lap, glancing up every few minutes to watch the mud-spattered produce trucks from the farmers' market and the glittering stream of cars on Five Mile grumble past the sign out front that read HUGE LAWN SALE TODAY. He sold everything in two days.

Now he'd found a gun, a discovery he hadn't anticipated. The weapon felt good in his hand, strong and weighty, significant in a way that made him feel confident of its ability to inflict great bodily damage. Evan tried spinning it on his finger, like the cowboys did in the western movies he'd watched as a boy on the living room couch, but the pistol slipped from his hand, bounced against his thigh, and clanged on the floor. The retired security guard in the condo below thumped weakly on the ceiling three times.

"Sorry," Evan hollered, and snatched the gun up. He brought it close to his face, close enough to smell the burnt residue of gunpowder at the end of the barrel. He took a deep breath.

"She never fired the thing," he whispered, suddenly confused. For a moment he pictured her crouched beside her bedroom door late at night with the pistol leveled at the entrance as someone attempted to jig the lock from outside. There wasn't any reason for her to have it in her possession. The building was equipped with security doors and alarm systems. Police patrolled her block three times a night. She'd even had him put two new deadbolts in her door almost fifteen years ago, before he'd left for college.

He shook his head, sat on the floor against the wall and rubbed his left knee. Her dying had been hard on his body. Going up and down the stairs so often had made his joints sore and puffy. Sometimes, in the late afternoons, he actually felt water collect in the muscles above his knee caps, a sensation that reminded him of the trout-filled streams they used to fish in the undeveloped counties west of the city.

"Be sure to give your line a little tug once you feel one hit your lure," she'd once whispered during a day of fishing on Orchard Lake. They were standing on the grassy banks beneath the willow trees.

"I know, Nan," Evan whined. "You've been telling me that since I was a kid. I haven't forgotten."

She nodded and squinted out over the water where sunlight glinted on its surface. "Then I suspect you'll catch our dinner tonight, right?"

She'd dipped the tip of her rod into the lake and flicked it upward so that water rained down on his head.

A few hours after discovering her first note two weeks ago, Evan happened upon another under the bathroom sink, tacked up behind the bottled hair dyes, shampoos, deodorants, toilet paper, boxes of Kleenex, and the plastic vials that contained the nitroglycerin pills she'd refused to take when the doctor first prescribed them.

Evan, there's $400 for you in one of my bureau drawers. I'm sure you'll find it. Use this money wisely. Maybe get your exhaust system fixed.

The small hairs on the back of his neck stiffened after he read this note. He'd folded the paper into a small triangular wedge and slipped it into his back pocket. How did she know he needed the money, he wondered, crunching the note further into his pocket with his thumb until the paper formed a small ball. He couldn't remember saying anything to her about it when she was alive, not even when they watched the Midas Muffler commercials during Lion games.

He peered at his face in the bathroom mirror. Crooked little lines jutted like veins beneath his eyes, the scars of many sleepless nights since her death. He stared at the floor, shook his head, and muttered a question he found unsettling: "Who was she?"

Clearly, she had expected to die sometime soon, Evan now realized as he stood in her bedroom under the fluorescent light fixture and studied the gun, clenching his hand around until the skin under his fingernails turned white. She'd reconciled herself to it. Maybe she sensed it the afternoon before as she sat on her sofa watching a Barney Miller re-run and massaging Ben Gay into her knuckles, a tiny knot of pain in her forearm growing longer and more intense as it crawled past her shoulder and settled deep inside her chest. She could have called; his apartment was only sixteen miles away. It wouldn't have taken him long to come over and drive her to the hospital.

He placed the gun on the bureau, shoved his hand into the stocking, and removed the bullets. He rotated the box in his hand and noticed a note taped to the outside, which he removed and placed on the bureau in front of him. It read

Evan, l have had this gun since the riots. You may have noticed that it's been fired—only twice, so please don't be angry with me. When I first bought it back before you were born, I fired it in the condo to get what the man at the store said was a feel for the gun. Then I fired it last May to make sure it still worked properly. On the wall behind my bedroom door, you'll find two holes right next to each other. I don't know how to fix them. As you can see, I've tried to cover them up with toothpaste over the years but they've caved in every time. Maybe you'd be a good boy and patch them before you sell the place.

If you decide to keep the gun, be sure not to keep it loaded in your apartment. I called around to some shops listed in the Yellow Pages. George's Guns on Five Mile and Newburg in Livonia will buy it back at a good price.

Take care and remember your vitamins every day, love Nan—

Evan folded up the note, stuffed it into his back pocket, and stared out the bedroom window. Down below, under the oak trees where blackbirds squabbled irritably from their nests, a few elderly people were stooped over their gardens. Mounds of weeds and clumps of dirt lay scattered on the cracked sidewalk.

He pushed the window open. The late summer air was cool and held the distant scent of freshly laid tar and burning leaves, a smell he always associated with his childhood in this neighborhood. The sun behind the office buildings across the street painted the feathery clouds with pink light. To the right of the building, cars hummed by on Five Mile.

He took a breath. It was almost fall. White tendrils trailed from the exhaust pipes of cars. He glanced at the pistol in his hand and wondered, just for a second, what it would be like to hold a loaded gun, to feel the cool barrel in his sweaty palm or pressed to the side of his head, to know that each bullet contained the power to pinch out life in a matter of seconds. He peered into the dark barrel. He placed it to the side of his head and moved it in circles in his hair, making sure his finger was planted firmly against the trigger guard as he stood near the open window. Finally Evan removed the gun, rested it on its side in his palm, looked down at it, and wondered how he should act now that she was gone. He pushed a hand through his hair and thought a moment. He wasn't sure what the pain was supposed to feel like; no one he'd known so well had ever died. What he might consider pain was kinked in his side like a cramp. Maybe the real ache would come later in life, perhaps on a Christmas Eve as he ate dinner alone at his kitchen table and watched snow flakes settle on the pine trees in the woods behind his apartment building.

"Alone," he whispered, fiddling with the empty cylinder on the pistol.

He stood a few seconds, feeling the air move in and out of his mouth. Finally, he picked up the box of bullets. His hand was unsteady and he dropped a handful of them on the floor. A few rolled toward the wall. Above the dark baseboard, he saw a tiny crack in the wall that spread upward to two holes the size of half dollars. He crouched and put an eye to one of the holes.

"Hello," he yelled, listening as his voice echoed behind the wall. It soon died away and was replaced by the vague drone and chinking of machinery in some other part of the building, maybe a washer and dryer running in the basement three stories below. He stuck his fingers into the holes and tried to touch the interior wall but he couldn't reach it. The air was cool and moist. He snapped off a few pieces of drywall around the hole, until one hole slightly larger than his entire fist developed. He wiped the chalky crumbs of plaster onto the floor beside the revolver.

He reached into his pocket, extracted his grandmother's notes, and dropped them into the hole. Then he picked up the box, poured the bullets into his cupped hand, dumped them into the holes, and listened as they clattered like drumsticks against the copper and metal pipes. The old man downstairs rapped on his ceiling and barked something Evan couldn't make out. Finally Evan picked up the gun and jammed it into the hole with his palm. The old man smacked his ceiling harder, sending pieces and crumbs of loose drywall to the floor.

"Sorry!" Evan hollered.

He went to her desk and took out a few sheets of scratch paper and a roll of scotch tape. He walked into the kitchen to where his tool box sat on the floor, reached in and removed his putty knife and can of spackling compound. He went back to the hole in the bedroom, crumpled the paper into balls, and stuffed them into the hole until they were flush with the surface. Replacing a square section of the drywall was the correct thing to do, but he didn't want to invest the time. He placed a few strips of tape over the hole. Using his thumb, he popped the top off the spackle can, scooped a thick, rich layer of the white goo with the knife and began smearing it into the hole.

"Sorry," he whispered, spackling over the hole until it was completely covered.

Standing Outside the D & C

The scar on his sister's wrist hadn't faded. Not entirely. James extended the photograph over the kitchen table, through a wall of sunlight that poured in from the sliding glass door, and squinted at Anne's image. She wore a gray sweatshirt one or two sizes too large, with the phrase Abbinton Catholic School for the Special printed in old English script across the front. Or was the name changed to Ebbington? He dragged an oily thumb across the picture, but the letters of the school name remained fuzzy. The focus was incorrect, he figured, rotating the photograph in his fingers. Or else the photographer hadn't properly adjusted the shutter speed on the camera before taking the photo.

He placed the picture on the table and raised his wrist in front of his face. He scanned the wrinkles, blemishes, spike marks from little league when he was a kid, and blue veins that zigzagged across the tissue beneath his skin, as if noticing the similarities between his and Anne's arm for the first time. Almost the same, he concluded, shifting his gaze from his wrist to Anne's and back again. Only a few minor differences: her veins looked bluer; the skin around her elbows was paler; her bones were noticeably thinner. Unlike her, stiff blond hair covered his arms and knuckles, and the cords of well-defined muscle that stretched from his hands to his elbows were as hard as planks of wood. He flexed his forearm, watching the muscle bulge against his bone. It was good for brothers and sister to have their own distinguishing characteristics.

He peered out the sliding glass door, making sure no one passing on the oak-lined road that ran in front of his yard could see him as he sat at his kitchen table, probing his wrist with a finger. After a moment he stopped prodding his skin and gently placed his wrist into his mouth. He moved it around a second or two, arranging the bone evenly between his upper and lower jaw, deciding which position felt most comfortable. He grunted, surprised at how easily it fit, then bit down, held his teeth in place and counted to three. His taste buds watered. With his tongue he stroked the underside of the bone, the skin and tissue soft like wet leather. Finally he removed his wrist, laid it on the tablecloth in front of him, and bent forward to examine his moist skin; two rows of indented and red teeth marks had emerged.

He shook his head and looked out the smudgy kitchen window, past the yard freckled with knots of barbed weeds and bright dandelions, until his eyes settled on a group of children entwined on the monkey bars in the park. From a distance they looked normal. James nodded at this observation, then glanced down at his kitchen table. Using his coffee spoon, he propped up the letter sent from Sister Mary, the head administrator from Anne's school. He'd already memorized some sentences: changes in medication required, increased need for verbal prompts, appetite above average, asks about mother.

Asks about mother. James took a sip of his cold coffee and sighed. Looking back, he remembered very little about her: the sound of her voice when she scolded him for drawing Dino from the Flintstones on the kitchen wall with a purple crayon, the lavender scent of her hands as she brushed away the hair that fell in front of his face, the meals she enjoyed cooking for them the most. He guessed that spaghetti and baked garlic bread was her specialty, since it was still one of his favorite meals. Minestrone soup and toasted bagels as well. Although he couldn't be sure, James believed she'd performed most motherly duties before she left: escorting them to the park during the warm afternoons; playing with them in the sandbox; making sure they didn't bury their new Barbie and G.I. Joe dolls in the muddy clay of their unfinished driveway after a rainstorm. It was easy to imagine her sitting at the end of his bed humming Elvis songs before tucking him in at night, her thin body silhouetted against the glow of hallway light that filled the doorway behind her.

He shook his head and looked down into his lap, realizing the difficulty involved in trying to piece together such a fragmented memory; he simply couldn't recall if his mother had done these things or not. By the time he was a senior in college, her leaving had become a brief flash of light against a dark backdrop, like the trail from a falling star he saw during a hunting trip in the Upper Peninsula of Michigan one fall weekend.

He picked up the photograph and studied it again. He and Anne hadn't seen her since the day she left in 1977 or 1978. James wasn't sure what year it was. Since then, she tried to let him know how she was doing, in one form or another. She sent birthday and Christmas cards the first few years after she was gone, with five and ten-dollar bills taped to the inside flaps. Beneath the bills sometimes lingered the red, blotchy imprint of her lips shaped into a kiss. The cards always arrived a few weeks late and without a return address. Once, after she'd been gone just over two years, she'd sent him Hank Aaron's rookie card in a special transparent plastic case, and a rubber tree plant for Anne—the first and only time she'd ever sent presents. For the most part she simply mailed postcards with aerial views of cities that sprawled and glinted for miles in all directions like Detroit, Chicago and New York, with the words "Thinking about you" scribbled in pencil across the back.

James kept every card and envelope she'd sent. Together, bound in piles with thick rubber bands and stacked one on top of another into a shoe box, they were the only real, tangible pieces of evidence he and Anne had of his mother's existence. When his father was away in Muskegon or Traverse City for business during the day, James liked to remove the shoe box from the closet shelf in his bedroom, unwrap the rubber bands, pour the cards on his Speed Racer bedspread, and press them one-by-one to his nose, trying to smell his mother's scent on every one. But that never worked: all he could ever smell was the dusty card stock and the dried smudge of ketchup or jelly still jammed beneath his fingernails from the lunch his babysitter had prepared for him and Anne. Or else he pieced together the disjointed and faded letters of town names stamped in the upper right corner by using his father's fountain pen from the study to fill in the broken lines. He made out a few names: Ann Arbor, Flint, Sturgis, Marquette, Munising Bay. Some towns were only a few miles from Northville where he and Anne grew up: Troy, Farmington Hills, even Novi, just down Beck Road, past the dusty horse farms and the green, overgrown apple orchards dotted with shiny red apples the size of racquetballs. But when he called information for the telephone number of a Sara Evinston in these towns, the operator could never locate a number under that name.

He leaned back in his kitchen chair, took a deep, uninhibited breath, and considered the humid summer afternoons he and Annie walked to town for lunch as children, strolling past the colonials with green belts of ivory braided around their white columns. That was a good memory, something he could focus on. Once they completed two or three miles of their journey, they stopped to rest and watch the swirling dust, kicked up by passing cars, blend with the humidity in the trees above. James smiled. He remembered how hard Anne concentrated on staying in a straight line behind him as he led them around the marshy pond, willow trees and knots of raspberry bushes, glancing back every few feet to make sure she didn't eat the unripened, dust-covered fruit hidden in the leafy shadows when he wasn't looking.

Once in town, where they pressed their faces against the window of the D&C and gazed at the new toys, James peered into the reflection of Anne's eyes in the glass and listened to her coo like a mourning dove when she'd realized they were only one block from the Dairy Queen. On those days he pretended she was a normal sister, the kind who sat next to him on the picnic tables in the parking lot outside Dairy Queen with her small, delicate fingers pinched between his, teaching her how to squeeze ketchup and mustard from packets onto a hamburger without making a mess.

He looked outside his window to see the children in the park untangling themselves from the monkey bars and bounding toward the thick woods at the edge. James contemplated the picture again. He studied the blank expression of his sister's face and gazed at her straight blond hair, the radiance of which seemed to have dimmed over the last four years. Physically, she looked older, which, he presumed with a stroke of a finger across her face, was natural. But her acne had become worse; dots of red pimples had formed two small circular patterns of equal size like a rash at the bottom of her fleshy cheeks.

He dropped the picture in a patch of sunlight on the table, slurped his coffee and looked out the window as the children in the park appeared from the shadows between the trees. "Make an appointment, idiot," he admonished himself aloud, trying to remember the exact number of months it had been since he'd seen her last.

He was twelve that Saturday she'd bit her wrist. He remembered the click of her teeth penetrating skin and the blood that saturated the sleeve of her pink Mickey Mouse pajama top. At first he figured she was throwing another fit to get something she wasn't allowed to have for breakfast—a bowl of cherry ice cream from the carton hidden behind the white, frosty packages of meat in the freezer, or some Doritos from the cupboard above the stove. Growing up, her capacity for junk food had always amazed James: her record for the most burgers consumed in one sitting occurred at Dairy Queen when he was eleven—three cheeseburgers and four hamburgers in an hour and a half. She ate everything. Sometimes while he and his father tossed the baseball back and forth in the front yard after school, Anne sat on the porch of their house eating bag after bag of Funyuns, Doritos and Munchos from the Frito Lay variety pack his father bought them for desert on his way home from work.

They'd grown accustomed to her fits if she wasn't allowed the things she wanted. Most times her outbursts were preceded by a moment of whimpering as she rocked back and forth in her high chair, her gaze fixed upon her lap, her left thumb planted firmly in her mouth. Hair pulling was one of her worst methods, especially when her second favorite treat—cherry ice cream with potato chips ground up into a fine powdery dust and sprinkled on top—was denied her.

The first time she'd enacted this method occurred during breakfast one weekend when he was 12. Anne had walked to the refrigerator and selected a container of strawberry ice cream from the freezer to start her day. His father, watching as she meticulously inserted her spoon beneath the lip of the cardboard top and pried it open, stood up from the table, snatched the ice cream from her hands and angrily stuffed it back into the freezer without its top.

"No," he barked. Anne glared at him. Then she raised her hand high above her, plopped it on her head, and deftly yanked out a small cloud of blond hair, which she deposited on the floor beside her feet. She had pulled so hard that James picked tiny flecks of dried blood from her scalp that night as he brushed her hair before bedtime.

The worst, however, was the morning she bit into her wrist and severed a vein. A small puddle of blood pooled on the plastic table cloth beneath her arm. James sat across from her, reading the back of his cereal box, unaware for several seconds of what she'd done. He glanced down at his bowl of Lucky Charms, scooped a few heaping spoonfuls into his mouth, then looked up and saw her wrist resting on the table. He spit his cereal back into his bowl, shot to his feet and stood a moment without moving. He was unsure what to do—telephone the doctor, or call down the road to Mr. Barnsby for help. An ambulance, he quickly surmised, searching for the phone hidden beneath the kitchen mess, might take too long.

James leapt out of his chair and lunged toward the sink. He grabbed a dirty kitchen towel off the counter, rushed over to Anne, wrapped it around her arm, and quickly searched the kitchen for something more to help. As his eyes raced from one kitchen corner to the other—over the mound of crusty dishes heaped in the sink, past the open jars of jam, peanut butter and orange marmalade strewn across the white Formica counter—he wanted to jump through the sliding glass door behind him and dash into the woods out back until he reached his fort in the grassy clearing along the edge of Paterson Creek. At least then things could be quiet for a little while.

Anne struggled to free herself from his grip.

"Sit down!" James screeched. She leapt to her feet and attempted to wrench her body between him and the ends of the towel. She almost broke free, but James held her right arm firmly and gave it a small squeeze, stopping her cold. In one succinct motion, he clasped the towel around her wrist with his left hand and pulled her to him. He leaned forward and hummed The Beatles' "Let It Be," a song that had always calmed her when she was younger. Anne stopped crying. She looked up at him, stared at a spot of skin above his left eye where a smudge of blood lingered, and began to coo.

"You're okay," he whispered, holding her tight.

His father arrived home just as James removed the towel to examine her wrist. Blood rushed to the surface of her wound, flooding the small, ragged tears in her flesh. He clamped the towel back down, then rubbed the top of her head.

"She bit her wrist again." He wiped his bloodied and shaking hands on his pajama top. "It's really bad this time."

His father squinted through his cigarette smoke and took her arm in his hand. He carefully peeled back the towel, then bent his head to make a closer inspection of her wound.

"Christ," he hissed, tightening the towel around Anne's wrist. "How long ago?" he asked. With his free hand he touched her cheek and rubbed away the streaks from her tears. Anne leaned her head against his hand. "You're okay, baby," he whispered.

"A few minutes."

His father stood up. He placed his hand on Anne's head and said, "She's gonna need stitches."

He walked over to the sink, turned on the faucet and placed his lit cigarette in the stream of water until the ember hissed and fizzled out. Then he dropped the butt into a small Tupperware bowl and zipped up his jacket. "Grab you're coat and let's get going."

"I have to go?" James asked, his hand now resting on Anne's shoulder. He kneeled in front of her, took her free hand in his, and quickly attempted to instruct her on how to apply direct pressure to her wound. Anne began to fidget.

"Don't ask why. Just get your coat and lets go."

"Dad," James whined. He glanced at his bowl of Lucky Charms. The pink, blue, yellow and red marshmallows were growing soggy in his milk. Sometimes, if Anne was seriously injured, he didn't mind driving to the hospital with his father, but on Saturday he liked to watch Bugs Bunny. Besides, he was still in his pajamas and felt shaky.

"You have to keep an eye on her while I drive," his father whispered through clenched teeth. "So get yourself together and let's go."

James brought his cup to the sink and rinsed it in a stream of hot tap water. Ten years, he thought to himself, recalling the last holiday his family was together. Christmas or Thanksgiving, 1995. Maybe Labor Day weekend, after his father flew north from South Carolina to play in a charity golf event sponsored by a Ford dealership in Dearborn. There was always some business meeting or golf event during the last few years that precipitated most of his father's visits to Michigan. On occasion, however, the school and state required his presence at annual review meetings to discuss Anne's progress in full detail. For these particular trips he made special arrangements to stay longer and visit with James.

James stuck his fingers into his mouth, sucked out the coffee grounds lodged beneath his fingernails, and spat them into the sink. Warm water bubbled over the rim of the cup as his hands diligently scrubbed. Once completed, he reached into the sink and hoisted another mug, its white porcelain surface spotted with faint coffee stains. He moved his palm around the cup, over tiny chips and cracks, the once-sharp edges worn smooth, and came to a simple conclusion: the distance he felt between himself, Anne and his father had no direct bearing on his present life. Families, he decided with little resignation, simply grew apart.

He jammed his fingers into the cup again until his knuckles burned with pain from the hot water, and briskly shook his head a few times, hoping to coax this thought from his mind. Still, no matter how hard he tried he couldn't deny the sense of incompleteness he often felt about his father and sister, especially after finding a stray picture of the three of them, taken during a holiday many years ago, on the dusty floor of his front closet. Sometimes it was the discovery of an old, yellowing postcard, wedged between a knot of unused athletic socks in back of a dresser drawer, that dredged this feeling into the open.

He looked around him, past the kitchen walls covered in a new coat of white paint, into the small, oak-paneled family room where several dirty glasses sat on the coffee table. Framed photographs of his sister and father rested in a wedge of sunlight on the fireplace mantle. He gazed out the window above the sink and traced the rolling contours and impressions of his yard and the park with his eyes. Once, maybe three years ago, just before the new sod was set in his back yard, he had dinner with his father at a restaurant during a visit. They spoke mostly about the Tigers and Red Wings. After a few beers and the arrival of their entrees, James said, "We should go see Anne while you're in town."

His father forked his roasted filet, diced a large piece with his steak knife, and delicately laid it into his wrinkled mouth before answering. "I might be tied up with my investment guy most of tomorrow and the next day," he explained, his eyes trained on the glassed candle resting in the center of the table. "It's been more than a year since I saw her last. She might not be too receptive, especially since she started on this new medication."

"Phone call can fix that," James suggested, "that would help."

His father snatched his napkin from his lap and brought it to his lips. "It's taking a little time for her to get used to the new medication," he said, swallowing a mouthful of food. "Sister Mary mentioned that Anne's been forgetting simple things lately, like brushing her teeth or cleaning up her work area in the shop when she's through for the day. One night she even got up and unlocked the main doors in the school for no reason. It's all in the copy of that report I sent you last week."

James picked up his fork. "I haven't read it yet," he admitted, taking a quick bite of chicken. "Maybe it would do her a lot of good if we called. Maybe seeing her might be too much, but a phone call could help."

"I've thought of that. Numerous times, Jimmy. Unfortunately, calling or going to see her right now might bring back too much at one time," he said, studying James' face. "Sister Mary's report says that Anne is starting to remember certain events that happened years ago, things that normal people tend to forget or lock away in the back of their minds. Apparently Anne's been asking where your mother is." He returned to his food. "You should read it."

James peered down at his plate, trying to avoid a discussion about the report. Using his fork, he plowed his steamed carrots into the puddle of brown teriyaki sauce, paused, then asked, "Was she sick during her pregnancy? I mean, did something happen when she was carrying Anne? A fall, maybe?"

His father shook his head and hesitated a moment. "No," he said. "Nothing like that. Back then there were just some things doctors couldn't quite understand or figure out right away."

"She was sick then?"

His father clutched his napkin and paused, as if hobbled by James' inquiry.

"It was a difficult pregnancy," he confessed. "She was nervous with Anne. Always on edge and moody. Not that it's uncommon or abnormal for a pregnant woman to feel that way."

He slid back in his seat and rested a moment. "Your mother had a tough ride, so the doctor prescribed some tranquilizers. Sometimes I'd give her a little wine before bed just to take the edge off. You know, make it easier for her to fall asleep, that sort of thing. But then she started drinking the wine a little more often, sometimes two, three nights a week." He shook his head and narrowed his eyes. "One day, when you were almost two, I came home in the middle of the afternoon. She was drunk and sitting on the couch in the living room with you curled up in her arms, staring out at the street during a rainstorm. She was close to seven months pregnant by then."

He leaned over his plate. "It was a tough time. Things were never that great between us. Uneasy."

"Uneasy?" James asked.

"Yes," his father said and clenched his jaw. "It took nearly two years to find out about Anne. We had to have special tests done, make certain arrangements for her. Your mother couldn't accept it." His eyes wandered away from the table a moment. "I guess neither of us knew what to do."

He picked up his knife and fork, chiseled a slice of filet, and pondered the candle in the center of the table. The glow of the flame made his eyes look bloodshot and heavy with memory. "Your mother always wanted a daughter," he concluded, his jaw muscles working in synchronized rhythm as he chewed his steak. "But I don't think she was completely ready for the responsibility Anne required."

After the dishes, James hopped into his car and drove to Anne's school. He watched in the rear view mirror as columns of dust rose over the dirt road and the cornfields stubbled with young husks. Chunks of loose gravel and rock rattled and chinked under his fenders, then spun off and thumped into the dried out ditches on both sides of the road. After a few miles he guided his Chevy past a thick wall of pines, spruces and brown scrub brush, until the squat, red -bricked buildings of the school emerged to his right, hunkered down into a small valley.

He pulled to the shoulder in front of the parking lot and sat a few minutes studying the main administration building, with its sprawling front porch, two rows of white-pained windows, and red-brick facade. An impossible place for an institution, way out here in the middle of nowhere. No police or fire stations, no place for a public phone. Except for the obligatory electrical pole and speed limit sign stabbed into the dirt that ran along the roadside, there was little to indicate that cars regularly drive through this area. James turned and faced the direction from where he came, paused, then looked across a green meadow to his right and finally up the rolling stretch of road that lay ahead of him and the school. No homes or farms set back under the tall oak trees like a normal countryside, or carved into a field. Nothing but the school.

He steered his car into the circular drive and parked in front of the administration building. Inside, a small brown-haired woman sat at a desk behind the reception counter with several phones in front of her. One receiver was pinched between her head and thick shoulder; she raised a tiny sausage finger to let James know she knew he was there. On her desk was a nameplate with the word Edie Jones inscribed in gold lettering. James waited, listening as she answered another volley of calls and placed people on hold. Finally she smiled at James and hung up the receiver. With a grunt she hefted her pear-shaped body from her desk and waddled over to him.

"Can I help you?"

"Yes, I'm here to see Anne Evinston."

"And you are?"

"Her brother," he said. "Jim Evinston."

"Okay," the woman sighed and quickly plunged her hands beneath the counter. She removed a ledger and placed it in front of her, licked her finger and thumbed through pages swiftly, stopping at what looked to be Anne's name, along with several penciled notes near the right edge of a page.

"It's kind of an unexpected visit," he said, watching the top of the woman's head as she studied the ledger. "I'd like to see her. My company's transferring me to Ohio and I don't know when I'll be back."

"Um hum," she murmured, still reading. Finally her head stopped moving. "It says here that Anne is helping Sister Mary today in her apartment out back. Some cleaning chores." She squinted up at James. "It also says Anne's not to have any unexpected visitors right now."

James nodded. "Maybe an exception can be made."

He watched the woman, whose squinting gaze was fixed on his face. "Let me call Sister Mary."

She waddled back to her desk and plucked a phone receiver. She held it to her ear, dialed, waited a second or two, then began talking rapidly. After a few nods of her head and several um-hum's, she hung up the phone and waddled back to the reception counter. She folded her chubby hands together and attempted a smile.

"Mr. Evinston, Sister Mary feels it's not a good time to visit with Anne. She's encountering a difficult period right now and Sister worries that Anne might become a little more excitable or confused."

James tapped his finger on the counter. "I can't see her for just a few minutes?" he asked, bewildered by the sudden mix of relief and disappointment he now felt. "I'm leaving in a few days and don't know when I can get back again. If you'd like, you and Sister Mary can be in the room."

She pursed her thin lips and stared down at the ledger, still clutched in her hands, as if considering this concession. Finally she shook her head. "I *am* sorry."

James nodded. He stood quietly in front of her, nodding over and over.

"I should have called," he sighed. "The transfer happened so fast, I didn't have time to think of all of the things I had to get done." He looked away and down the hall. "Can I see her later? Another month?"

Edie nodded. "Of course." She opened the ledger and ran a finger down a line of dates. "August looks open. Would the seventh be good? One-thirty or two?"

"That's fine," James said. "Two is good."

Edie pencilled in his name and closed the binder. She drummed her fingers on the cover and smiled up at him. "Anne's doing well, Mr. Evinston. She just needs to continue with her new meds a little longer before she's ready for visits again."

James dug into his pocket for his car keys. "August 7," he whispered to himself and walked through the front door to the parking lot.

The sisters' apartments were attached to the rear of the administration building in a single row of six. At the north end of the row, positioned in front of where James stood, sat the mail slots for each apartment, encased in a square wood frame and supported by a thick beam cemented into the ground. He ran a finger along the names taped to each aluminum door until he located Sr. Mary Tarmissa #2.

James peered down the walkway. The second apartment—eight, maybe ten feet away.

He clenched his jaw, took a long breath, and forced his body toward Sister Mary's apartment. Once in front of her door, he brought his face close to the screen and quietly gazed inside. Symphony music played low on a radio. Hunched against the far wall sat a brown leather couch. Above it, the yellow drapes that covered the window diffused sunlight, giving the apartment an antique, ethereal glow.

"Anne, please put the bread in the fridge for me," Sister Mary said from somewhere inside the apartment, her voice steady and firm. Anne grunted, a sound he'd never heard from her before. A husky, formidable grunt. "That's a good girl."

A few dishes clanked. The refrigerator made a sucking sound when it opened and condiment bottles clanged when it was closed.

"Be a good girl and sponge the counter," Sister Mary said.

Anne grunted again. James moved forward, his palm pressed hard against the door and tried to listen for the wet slurp of the sponge against the counter as she cleaned the kitchen. He imagined her pushing appliances aside and drenching the corners that Sister Mary may have forgotten over the years, then shifting to the refrigerator to expunge the smudgy fingerprints from its surface. He leaned his head against the doorframe, feeling his resolve suddenly swirl, then ebb and slowly fade. Sweat beaded on the back of his neck and he rubbed it away. Until now, it wasn't fully clear to him how deeply his uncertainty lingered when faced with visiting Anne. On most days it was simpler to believe that his presence was inessential and easy to discount, as if he were a distant relative his family hadn't seen or heard from in over twenty years.

James raised his head off the door frame. He glanced inside the apartment, listening again to dishes clinking, then slowly backed away from the door. He crept past the two apartments, turned left at the mailboxes. When he stopped moving, he found himself crouched behind a bush that afforded a good view of the sisters' apartments without revealing his position at the edge of the cement parking lot.

With his hands cupped around his eyes like binoculars, he surveyed the apartments. His eyes roamed the doorways, the red brick facades and windows of each dwelling, until he heard the whine of a screen door opening and the sound of it slapping closed. Then, from the shadow of the second apartment, Anne emerged, clutching a brown grocery bag close to her chest. She wore a pair of white tennis shoes, dark Bermuda shorts and blue Mickey Mouse t-shirt two sizes too large. She walked swiftly to the dumpster at the far side of the parking lot. When she reached it, she slid the metal door open, stood back a foot or two, waved away a cloud of flies swarming at the opening, then deftly heaved the bag into the dark space. She slid the door closed and trotted back.

James shook his head and frowned. From a distance, Anne appeared to be doing well; she didn't scowl or appear crippled by depression as the receptionist had suggested. In fact, he sensed an evenness of control he hadn't noticed in the years before Anne had been enrolled in school: her eyes remained steadily fixed on the rusty, fly infested dumpster before her as she carried out the chore presented to her by Sister Mary.

He stood back, pushed a branch away from his face and waited a few seconds before calling her name. "Anne." She continued walking to Sister Mary's apartment. He cupped his hands around his mouth. "Anne," he blurted, his voice echoing against the exterior walls of the dumpster.

She turned before stepping into the shadow of the roof overhang and squinted in his direction. Behind her, the hinges of the screen door whined. Sister Mary emerged, a wrinkled hand raised to shield her eyes from the sun. She was a tall woman with straight white hair to her shoulders. From a distance, her smooth cheeks looked to have been chiseled out with a spoon, giving her face a grave, melancholic expression. She wore gray dress slacks, a pair of white tennis shoes and a white button-down shirt with the sleeves rolled evenly to her elbows.

"Who is that?" she demanded, examining the grounds with a succinct turn of her head, uncertain from which direction his voice traveled. Anne looked at James and began to point. She took one step forward.

He moved to the edge of the bush. "It's Jim Evinston," he said. "Anne's brother."

Sister Mary gazed at the bush, her hand still held above her eyes. She gently laid her other hand on Anne's elbow and squeezed it in an attempt to direct her back to the apartment door. Anne didn't move.

"Out there, behind the bush?" she asked. "Mr. Evinston, this is very odd," she shouted, clutching Anne's arm. "Edie should've explained to you Anne's situation. Today's not a good day."

"I understand," James called back, still concealed by the bush. "I just wanted to see how she's doing. It's been a long time." He cocked his head. "She seems to be doing well."

Sister Mary nodded. From the bush, James could see her wilted biceps tense as she struggled to restrain Anne. "Please, Mr. Evinston," Sister Mary rasped, "today is not a good day for a visit. We cannot allow any disruptions in Anne's program. None."

James pursed his lips and considered the old woman's plea. He studied Anne straining against the Sister's hold, imagining her as a little girl, cooing while they stood in front of the D and C viewing the new toys. From where he stood now behind the bush, Anne looked like a normal person.

"Anne," he whispered. He stepped in her direction, but stopped, uncertain of which direction to move.

"Please, Mr. Evinston. You should leave now," Sister Mary warned, jostling to gain a better grip.

"I know," James whispered, acknowledging her caution with a nod, then started forward, his eyes fixed on Anne as she slowly pulled Sister Mary toward him.

III

Accomplices

His father's tool and die shop is finally gone. Alberts unhooks his flashlight from his gun belt, presses the button and pans the light over the oily foundation, past the spurt of weeds growing in the cracks, their green stems stubbled with white furry barbs. Once, not so long ago, his father made him work Saturdays in the shop, dredging oil and hydraulic fluid from the floor with industrial strength soap and a mop until the surface reflected the gauzy windows above where sunlight poured in and crows could be seen gliding back and forth across the sky like black smudges. He holds a hand close to his face and studies his cuticles. They're pink and healthy, somehow left unscathed from all those years of hard work and oil, the days when he slit his fingers on the rusted edge of a table and felt the blood run warm over his skin, or watched his thumb bloat red after dropping a fifteen-pound press block on it.

He turns his hand over and reviews the thick dark hair on the back side, then brings his hand forward again and inspects his cleaned fingernails more closely. He remembers the oily gunk that got trapped beneath them like a second layer of skin after cleaning the floor, and how he would coax it out with an eacto knife, digging precariously under the nail until a tiny slice opened on his soft skin and filled with blood. Nothing worked. Small screwdrivers, folded corners of shop orders, even toothpicks weren't able to remove the gunk. Sometimes gasoline or turpentine burned some of it away, but left dark stains on the backs of his hands and infections that burned deep inside the wounds weeks later.

Still, the work wasn't too bad, he decides, resting his hand on his arm and moving it back and forth so he can feel the long ribbon of his biceps form into a ball when he flexes. He can't fault the old man for that. Moving broken, gut-rusted machines out to the back yard behind the trees with nothing but an old rickety dolly, sweeping out the shop on Saturdays, getting rid of all that built-up oil—everything Alberts did gave him strength and helped define his character. He likes to believe that part of his existence was shaped by the work he performed, nourished by the sweat that caked the back of his neck and seeped down into his shorts when he was a boy. He continues touching his arm, squeezing and pinching the knot of muscle until a pain begins to settle deep into the fibers. A car turns down the street, accelerates, then speeds past the shop, its headlights spilling across the weedy lawn so that they illuminate Alberts standing in his affected posture, probing his muscles.

Beyond the shop foundation, at the end of his father's property where leafy vines have braided themselves around a wall of tree trunks and machinery, the glow of suburban light reflects in the low clouds above the outskirts of Detroit. When he was young and had finished cleaning the oil from the shop floor, Alberts sometimes climbed those trees and stared at the hazy outlines of distant buildings for hours, watching sunlight glimmer off the highest windows in the Renaissance Center just before sundown, thinking that some day that mass would spread until it consumed his father's shop and extend beyond the town where he and his father had lived. He passes his light over the trees and weeds in the backyard, then over the hewn mounds of dirt and sod sprinkled along the foundation where bulldozers gripped and uprooted the ground before driving into the crumbling walls. The rusty steel beams that had once jutted from the concrete floor and stretched to the ceiling are gone. They were plucked months ago by the iron jaw of a crane that swooped down from high above the trees, clutched the beams between its teeth and ripped them out with a smoky grunt of its diesel engine.

Alberts takes a step backwards and reassess the area where he stands. Crickets sing cheezit in the tall grass to his right. He looks back at the areas where the beams had once been evenly spaced apart along the pale wall like a rib cage, wondering what they'll be made into once they're melted down. He stands rigid, remembering a time he scrubbed rust from those beams with a wire brush and bucket of gasoline on a sunny Saturday afternoon. He was only twelve or thirteen. His father, standing behind him with his arms crossed over his round stomach, had said, "All that rust needs to come off before OSHA comes in next week."

Alberts hadn't looked up to acknowledge his father's words. He was too tired and sore and didn't want to expend the last drops of energy he had left. A moment passed;

finally his father stepped forward and tapped him on the arm to get his attention. He pointed a thick finger at the ceiling and said, "Even at the top, where the ceiling and metal meet. You can use the hydraulic lift to get at them."

Alberts dropped his brush into the bucket of gasoline, listening to it *kerplunk* and spit a few drops over the edge. He stared directly above him to where his father pointed. An orangish bubble of rust was visible and had attached itself to the seam where the beam and ceiling met. A few feathery layers had begun to branch out in a small arch across the ceiling. "You gotta get all that shit off. Use a putty knife if you have to," his father directed, staring at the ceiling.

"I know, I know," Alberts muttered. He rubbed his forearms, trying to soften up the muscle, his gaze still fixed on the beams above.

His father looked at him, his mouth tightened and eyes narrowed, as if studying a hunk of newly machined metal for flaws. "Well, there's an extra ten in it for you if you do a good job. If you need a hand with the lift, let me know. I'll be in the office." He started to walk back to the office at the other end of the greasy shop, hesitated, then turned around. He stared at the floor in front of Alberts and said, "If I haven't mentioned it, you're doing a good job." He turned again and continued toward his office, past a wall crowded with tables.

Now all that remains of his father's shop is dirt and concrete. Even the clay has been dredged from deep within the earth.

At the space where the door rested, Alberts crouches and slowly begins to fiddle with the soil, pinching it between his thumb and forefinger, feeling the bits of rock stick to his skin. Most of the soil is dark and rich, perhaps good enough for a farm or large garden. He plunges his fingers deeper, thinking he'll touch those first grains of sand that his father dug his shovel into the day he'd started building the shop, or his fingers will glide over the butt of a cigarette the old man might have smoked during a break from working. Alberts gazes up at the mist in the surrounding trees, trying to remember if his father smoked when he was young: he presses a finger to his temple and rubs, but his recollections of early childhood are undefined, as if he's awakened from a deep sleep and can only remember fuzzy shadows—his father and a woman he once dated lingering in the doorway of his room, smoking cigarettes and staring down at him while he slept. He continues digging in the dirt, forming a smooth trench, feeling the bits squeezing up under his fingernails, packing in tight until there isn't any more room for another speck. He concentrates a few seconds with his eyes closed, trying to summon his father's ghost from the haze so he can ask him how it feels to have his history wiped clean from the world.

The radio in his squad car squawks behind him and drowns out the sound of crickets. Alberts takes a few deep breaths, stands up, and walks back to the unit idling on the street. He slumps into the seat, closes the door, puts the car in gear and drives down the street. He glances back at the shop foundation and mounds of dirt, then further to the trees in back where a bead of a distant light reflects off a piece of abandoned machinery. No more history left. Just concrete and dirt smattered on an oil-stained floor.

As he drives, he catches a glimpse of himself in the window and turns to look. For a split second he recognizes his father's face in the glass—the tight-lipped mouth, sockets shrouded in shadow, the pale, blotchy skin hemmed in by dark brown curls. This recognition only lasts a moment, though; when he turns to face the window completely, his father's face is replaced by the points of white light that blink between trees and the empty lots. Don't look at all like him, Alberts whispers to himself, clenching his fist against the steering wheel.

He raises his hand and opens it. At least he inherited his hands, he decides, feeling a tiny spot of emptiness grow inside his stomach. He closes and opens his fist once more, then looks down at the hardened skin and red knuckles that have emerged over the years. The old man loved to use his hands when he spoke. During Fourth of July parties at the neighbors', after drinking too many cans of Schlitz Malt Liquor and eating all that Polish sausage, he'd sometimes sputter on about passing the business down to his son. He'd raise his big pale hands in front of him and spread them over the heads of the drunk neighbors like a preacher at some outdoor revival, suggesting the growth he'd achieve some day with Alberts running the business while he played golf in Florida or lounged on the deck of some cruise ship in the Caribbean.

Alberts listens to the drone of tires on pavement, trying to forget those parties. He moves through the intersection at 15 Mile and Coolidge where a dot of green light from the traffic signal shimmers on the greasy pavement. He pulls up at a 7-11 where several late night robberies have taken place in the last four years. The headlights of the car roam across the faded gray tar of the lot and come to rest on the curb. A young boy hunches over The Detroit Free Press stand. He jerks the handle with small, violent thrusts that cause the metallic door to echo against the houses across the street and throughout the quiet neighborhood. The boy wears a blue and black Troy High School varsity jacket. He doesn't turn around when Alberts pulls up and parks.

Alberts steps out of the car. "Hey," he barks. The boy swings around and Alberts hits his face with the through his fingers. "What's going on?" Alberts inquires.

"I can't see," the boy murmurs. With a fist, Alberts taps the handle of the light, realigning the beam until it's centered in the middle of the boy's chest. The boy puts his hands down and squints at Alberts. His cheeks are fleshy and dotted with pimples.

"You buying a paper?" Alberts asks.

The boy shakes his head. "Just checking out the front page. "

"Pretty late to be out."

The boy shakes his head and rolls his eyes. "I'm coming home from work," he sighs. "I work at the Burger King on Orchard Lake."

Alberts chews on this a little, holding the boy frozen in the light until he can sense the youth's nervousness start to subside. The radio squawks once, twice, three times as the dispatcher mutters something Alberts doesn't quite get. "Burger King doesn't close until three," he explains.

The boy looks into the light and holds up his hands. "My manager let me out early. You can call him if you want. Besides, I was only looking at the paper."

"Well, I could hear you looking at the paper half a mile away," Alberts says. He taps the spotlight again with his fist, until the beam is directly below the boy's chin. Between the lapels of his jacket, Alberts can see the amber t-shirt the boy wears, stained with dark spots, possibly from spattered grease. "Come here," Alberts instructs the youth and steps away from the car door.

The boy walks slowly over to Alberts. "Let's see some I.D."

He pushes a hand into his back pocket and produces a thin wallet, from which he extracts a smudgy driver's license. An odor emanates from his clothing. Alberts lifts his head, sniffs the air between the two of them a few times, deciding if the kid smells like pot, beer, or some kind of food he's spent all night preparing. He holds up the boy's I.D and shines his flashlight on it. James Morris. 2367 Wattles, Troy, Michigan. A decent neighborhood. Lots of families.

Alberts hands the license back to the boy. "I hope I don't catch you looking at the paper like that again."

"I was—"

Alberts holds up a hand to stifle the boy's protest and waves it in front of him. "Don't try to tell me what I saw," he says. "Just refrain from doing it again."

The boy stands there without speaking, gazing impatiently to his right where the buttery light shines down on his Ford Pinto. The passenger door is flecked with bright orange spots of rust.

"What would your parents say if they got a call saying their boy was in jail for attempting to steal a fifty-cent paper?" Alberts asks. "Fifty-cents. You think they'd like that?"

The boy shakes his head. "My father's asleep. He'll just let the machine answer."

Alberts looks back down at the boy's I.D. "Wrong answer," he murmurs, shaking his head. "I can always wake your father up. I bet he'd like to know what you're doing out this late screwing around with a newspaper stand. If I were you, I don't think my father would be too thrilled about my actions, especially if I show up at his door. Right?"

The boys' eyes widen. "I guess," he whispers.

"What's that?" Alberts blurts. "Speak up."

The boy lets out a heavy breath and stares down the street. "I'm sorry I shook the thing. I promise it won't happen again." He nervously looks at his car, then back to Alberts. "Can I please go?"

Alberts stands quietly, sizing the boy up. Short, wide shoulders, blond hair cut close to his scalp. An athlete of some sort. He's got the shoulders for football, maybe the legs for soccer. Finally Alberts hands over the boy's I.D. and nods. The boy walks to his car, steps in, starts it up and begins gunning the engine. Black and gray smoke huffs from his tail pipe and swirls in the hazy parking lot light. A section of rusty fender flaps against the wheel well. Alberts yells to the kid to open his window, but because of the bubbling hack of the exhaust system and the fender vibration, the kid doesn't hear him. Alberts shines his flashlight into the Pinto. The boy opens his window and scowls.

"Better get that exhaust fixed," Alberts says. "Liable to get a ticket."

The boy nods, raises a hand to respectfully acknowledge Alberts, then rolls the window up and leaves the parking lot. His car huffs and coughs all the way down Coolidge, the white smoke spitting from the exhaust in long tendrils. Finally, the car taillights disappear under the beads of streetlights.

Kids, Alberts thinks, shrinking back into his seat. He wonders what the boy's father will say when his son comes in late, reeking of hamburger grease and acting edgy. What if the father just doesn't care? Alberts shakes his head and depresses the gas pedal a few times, listening to the deep hum of the engine. No matter how uninterested fathers and mothers are in the lives of their children, they're bound by instinct to feel some degree of love. At least Alberts likes to think so.

He releases a mouthful of air and looks behind him before backing out. What if—what if. Lately he's been measuring his existence by this phrase—what if his mother hadn't passed away before his second birthday; what if he hadn't worked in the shop on Saturdays; what if he hadn't attended college; what if he took over his father's business; what if he'd been closer to the old man. Some days he finds it difficult to attach meaning to the questions, or to understand why he often feels alone in the world. But this doesn't bother him very often or for long periods; being alone is a fact he's grown accustomed to. Besides, he's got his job and that's what counts the most.

He peers into his rear-view mirror, puts the car in gear, drives out of the parking lot and continues with his patrol.

His spotlight slides across the weathered boards of the old fruit stand. Shadows in the empty door bend away from the light and disappear, revealing milk crates and glinting bottles strewn on the wood floor inside. Two foldout chairs spotted with rust and half hidden by a mass of green barbed weeds sit side by side out front.

A week ago he drove up to the building during his round and watched the silvery flash of studs from a leather jacket zip past the doorway as the kids escaped out the hole in the back wall and ran through the field, leaving behind an artery of trampled field grass and a cloud of cigarette smoke that hovered in the rafters. He got into his squad car, drove past the building, stopped, then stood on the front bumper of his cruiser and stared at the black tree line, watching as the glow of their cigarette embers danced between the tree trunks like fireflies.

He hasn't actually seen them face to face. At night in his cruiser, with his fingers tapping out a rhythm on the steering wheel and his eyes probing the shadows between the stores and gas stations, he imagines what they look like just from the things they leave behind: cigarette butts smeared with purple lipstick, used condoms strung from the rafters, beer bottles scattered in the corner. Sometimes an old *Playboy* or *Cosmopolitan* stuffed in a hole on the wall to keep out light. There is a girl—this Alberts is sure of—young, overweight, the sides of her head shaved and tinted blue. He envisions a tiny mole lingering at the corner of her pouting mouth. And then the two boys with army-green vests and tennis shoes that slap the pavement when they run from Alberts' light. Their parents have no idea where they are or what they do on Saturday nights.

Tonight, however, Alberts can't see any movement. He slides his spotlight over the chipped yellow boards and the shattered glass that glitters in the doorway. He cranks the car window down, turns his head until his ear is angled toward the shack, listens intently, but all he can hear is the whir of crickets in the fields around him.

He drives down Big Beaver Road with an unworried stare. The radio hums, then crackles, and the voice of the dispatcher—thick, marred from smoking—announces an accident at Adams and Charring Cross, three miles from Alberts position. He radios in, then increases the cruiser's speed until the engine grows louder and he's moving steadily faster toward the highway overpass. He passes a chewed up raccoon on the side of the road, an explosion of glass to the right of the cement and then, as his speed picks up, the flicker of white tennis shoes on the dirt shoulder. He peers into the rear view mirror, taps the break to illuminate the dry brush of the world behind him and the fragments of shattered bottles embedded in the dirt shoulder.

He turns around, then radios in that he's going to check on something, and heads back up the street. He drives along the shoulder, angling the car headlights until they slide across the mound. Slowly, out of the dark, the feet emerge, then a hand and finally the head with an arm wrapped around its neck and clearly out of joint. A clump of grass on the edge of the dirt shoulder conceals the youth's face.

Alberts pulls the car up within fifteen feet of the body and stops. He straightens the spotlight so that the youth's right side is completely illuminated. A few miles away the wail of a distant patrol car rises above the hum of crickets. From his seat behind the wheel, he can see the boy's light blond hair and the moist brown clumps of dirt plastered to his scalp. A pool of blood is smeared across his chest and darkens his tee shirt. Alberts angles the spotlight to light the area behind the body and washes the dirt shoulder in light; he sees nothing except the heavy remains of tire imprints from a truck or other vehicle.

He opens the cruiser's door, inhales deeply, then presses his feet to the ground and walks slowly to the body. Once in front of it, Alberts kneels and examines the wounds rimmed with dried blood. A sliver of vomit crawls its way up his throat as his fingers hover above the ragged holes in the boy's t-shirt. With a quick swallow, he forces it back down.

Finally Alberts stands and heads to his car. He opens the door and slumps into the seat, then snatches the microphone. "This is one-eleven," he says, squinting at the body. "I'm at Big Beaver near the 75 overpass. Got a body here. Looks like a shooting."

"Roger, one-eleven," the dispatcher says, then calls other units to the scene.

Alberts wanders into the field surrounding the scene to comb for evidence, stepping through short clots of burr bushes that claw his legs. Tangles of shadows twist and turn between the bushes as he moves into and out of the spotlight. He stares at the trees across the field for several minutes, at the shadow of the old fruit sand a fifty yards away, then trudges back to the car. A moment later a unit screams out of the west, startling the dead night with its high-pitched wail, and parks parallel to Alberts' car. The officer steps out—round-chested, heavy black mustache above thin bottom lip, forty-two, maybe forty-three-years-old, patches of gray sprinkled throughout his hair. He marches over to Alberts' side.

"Alberts," he says, his voice thick and raspy, the hectic eruption of red and blue light reflecting in the lenses of his glasses. "Shooting?"

"I, ah—some boy," Alberts manages, flicking a hand out toward the body. Another grainy clot of vomit attempts to climb up his throat, but again he suppresses it. "Can't be more than nineteen," he says, taking a deep, warm swallow. "Capped at least twice from what I can tell."

The officer stomps over to the boy, crouches down, and studies the body. He extends his meaty forefinger over the boy's nose without touching it, flicks a bug away, then peers into the bloodied chest.

"Well," he sighs, looking into the fields. "Scene unit on the way, right?"

"Yeah," Alberts says. He steps out of his car and stands at the door. Other units come racing down the street from the east, kicking up dust at the end of the road, their flashers swirling in the clouds like colored tornadoes. The officer, crouched at the boy's body, says, "I'd say seventeen at the most."

The road remains closed for three hours. The scene detectives shift the boy's body: the right half of his face looks similar to a pancake covered in strawberries. The clear areas of skin below his eyes are bruised and have begun to turn black and green. A toothpick of splintered bone protrudes from his skin in the area where his cheek, now a deflated balloon, once stood firm. His somber eyes are open, clear balls of blue water surrounded by threads of red. Part of his scalp is folded up; a three-inch section of cracked skull is visible, glossed over with a layer of blood. They outline his body with white tape before preparing him for the morgue wagon.

A few officers explore the fields with flashlights, studying the ground around the scene, their bodies bent at the waist, hands pulling and spreading bushes and field grass apart as they search for the gleam of shell casings or any other evidence. Two officers pour white plaster from a plastic pitcher into the tire tracks behind the boy's body and wait, crouched like baseball catchers, for the liquid to dry. All they've recovered have been the things found in the boy's pocket: twelve dollars in singles, a folded piece of notebook paper containing a few crumbs of coke and two buds of marijuana wrapped in cellophane from a box of cigarettes.

Alberts sits in his car watching the investigation. He wants to help, but whenever he comes within a foot of the body a burning sensation erupts in his stomach, followed by the bile that rises in his throat, simmers in his nose and threatens his mouth with its presence. A tall sergeant, his face pock marked and pale, stands close by, drinking coffee from a styrofoam cup, a clip board pinched between his right arm and ribs. He turns his head away from the body now and again and looks at Alberts.

After a few minutes of staring at the kid, the sergeant says, "Probably coming home from a party."

Alberts nods but says nothing. A slight chatter emanates from the men busy working the ground around them, a hum that blots out the buzz of crickets. Someone among the group chuckles.

The sergeant asks, "This your first?"

"Um hmm."

The sergeant looks back at the scene and rocks forward. A moment of silence hangs between them. Finally the sergeant asks, "How long have you been with the department?"

Alberts continues gazing at the scene. "Seven years," he says.

"Hmm," the sergeant grunts. "I was on the force only two when I saw my first. I didn't like the feeling then, and I don't like it now."

He tips the cup to suck the last drops of his coffee. "Kid from Garden City killed himself on 75," he whispers, looking back over his shoulder at the overpass and pointing his cup eastward. He pauses. "Further down, of course. Walked in front of Greyhound in the middle of the night. Left a blood stain on the highway from March until August." He stares up at the sky a moment, seemingly burdened by another thought. "We never could find one of his feet."

Alberts looks away. "Too young," he says. "I've seen people in the morgue, you know, that kind of stuff—" He shakes his head. "But this. The kid looks normal. At least from here."

The sergeant nods. "Can't always tell," he says and nods towards the scene. "Seems to get worse as the years go on."

The sergeant glances at the men working in the field, holding up in their gloved hands twigs, wrappers, and beer bottles, all caked in dry mud. He takes a step forward, but then slowly turns to Alberts. "When I was younger we never had to deal with this kind of shit. There were murders in the city and all that, but never anything like this." He looks down at his feet a moment, shakes his head and chuckles. "Not so long ago I told my oldest boy to be careful when he goes over to Canada. Not to stop for gas in the city, stay clear of Woodward downtown late at night. Used to think that was enough."

Alberts glances up at the officer to say something more but the sergeant is already strolling over to the scene van to log the possessions found on the body. Alberts squints after him, into the headlights of an opposite unit until they become nothing more than fuzzy dots of white and the sergeant's body looks like a twig with hands and feet. Alberts wonders about the kid's parents. Perhaps he only has a father, who sits right now at his kitchen table in an undershirt eating a t.v. dinner, the eleven o'clock news on the small black and white television that rests on the kitchen counter in front of him. An anchor talks about a fire on the north side of Detroit that chars three apartment buildings. The man shakes his head and whispers, "What next."

The father glances around the kitchen table, into the dark doorways that lead to the living room and dining room. Sometimes, Alberts thinks, the man stands at the picture window of the living room with nothing on but his tee shirt and white boxer shorts, drinking a bourbon and ginger ale, watching the stars flicker above the golf course just beyond his yard. He might have one more drink, then another, and another until his arms feel weightless and he glides around the room as if dancing with a woman. Many times the man has stood at the window, waiting. Staring up at the stars so many nights in a row, he's learned the names of the constellations—Gemini, his son's sign, their glittering arms reaching for one another; Taurus and Scorpio directly opposite each other, their stubbornness hinging them together forever in the sky. Sometimes, when he's almost drunk and the carpet below his feet feels like wet grass from a spilled drink, he can see a pin-prick of light hovering in the sky between the stars, and he thinks there is nothing as pure as that single bead of light blinking down on him, or the taste of bourbon on his chapped lips.

Perhaps his son, driving home in his car, will recognize that star and feel something familiar about it. He'll wonder about its density, origin, and how the world in which he lives could possibly be one-thousandth the size of that star. When he walks through the garage door of his house and browses in the pantry for something to eat, his father will walk out of the darkened living room and into the kitchen, lit only by the dim light above the stove. He'll come from behind, moving his hand to the boy's shoulder. But he'll stop short and resign himself to just stand behind his son, allowing his fingers to hover in the space above him. The shadow of his hand will slink along the back of his son's neck, bending in the light until it looks as if he is actually stroking his hair, twirling it between his fingers as he did when the boy was a baby.

The boy will sense his father's presence and twist around quickly, his young face startled, flushed red from alcohol. He'll place the box of cereal or bag of chips on the counter and whisper, "Jeez, Dad, you scared the hell out of me."

The man will straighten up and ask, "What did you do tonight?"

His son will regain himself and return to his search of the pantry. He'll look behind tin cans of soup with peeled labels and stretch his arms to reach the chocolate candy bars above, hidden behind a brown, wilted bag of potatoes. Once he has the candy in his hands, he'll mutter, "Nothing much. Hung out with the guys down at the Pit."

Alberts sees the father's neck hair bristle when he hears the name of that bar. The man will clamp his arms around his body, shake his head, maybe raise a hand to his face and study the dirt still trapped beneath his fingernail from his garden out back. Once, when he walked by the den on a Saturday afternoon, he heard his son mention that bar while on the phone to a friend. The boy spoke of standing near one of the open windows along Jefferson the entire night, drinking beer and swearing at people walking by on the street. He called teenagers ass bags and the old people who lurched by stale farts. He studies the boy—short blond hair, webs of freckles around his nose and the edge of shadow lingering in his sockets, the flat, unobtrusive openness of his face. It's difficult for him to consider his son a troublemaker.

"Bit dangerous down there, don't you think?" he asks. "It's not like it used to be when I was young. Shooting rats down at the river was considered a bit too much in my day. You'd get thrown in jail for that stuff."

The boy continues eating, smearing chocolate on the tips of his fingers, bloodshot eyes straining to keep focused on his father's mouth. He'll open the refrigerator, take out the container of milk and put it to his mouth, leaving brown fingerprints on the plastic jug when he's through. He'll wipe his lips on his sleeve and tell his father as he leaves the kitchen, "Don't worry. There was six of us. No one screws with a group."

Three in the morning. Alberts can see the man wandering into the kitchen to get a glass of milk. When he removes the plastic jug from the refrigerator, he'll stare at the fingerprints from his son, the muddy residue of chocolate smeared on the plastic handle, and measure their density with his drunken eyes. His thumb will linger above the prints, but he won't rub them away.

Later he'll stumble into his bedroom, sit on the foot of his bed, then slowly lay his body down. He'll think of the woman he's to take out this weekend, wondering if his boy will at least be around so that he can offer him a chance to go to the country club with them and eat a good meal instead of all that fast food. Get him to stop drinking for a night. Maybe take a break from going downtown again and trying to cause trouble.

Upstairs in the loft he hears his son's muffled cough. He'll listen more intently, searching the deafening black of his doorway for a reason to go to his boy and ask if he needs anything just as he had when his son was three. The man will concentrate on a small circular patch of white light in the hallway that appears to hover on the tufts of carpet. After a moment, silence will return. The air conditioner will click on and heave cool air out the duct opposite his bed.

"He'll straighten out," the man will whisper to himself.

He'll catch himself talking to the night again, his hands making large sweeping gestures above his body. He'll turn to the side and stare out one of the bedroom windows that face the fairway, but he'll not see detail in the course, only the black silhouettes of trees and rises in the apple orchard across the way. He'll envision the numbed, uninterested eyes of his son reflected in the window when the man brings home another girlfriend for his boy to meet; a blond with dark roots and a rear packed so tightly into her leather skirt that when she speaks her voice is faint. She will extend a hand toward the boy, offering some measure of friendliness, and the boy will take it, saying, "Nice to meet you."

And then, to his father, eyes averted, he'll mutter, "I'm taking off now."

This woman is not permanent, the man might reason to himself. These days it's very difficult to find permanence in anything.

From his bed, he'll see a light from an airplane far away in the eastern sky, glowing in the clouds above the trees on the fifth hole—red, blue, then white flashes. Sleep will creep toward him and his eyes will feel heavy, but still he'll search for that light above the trees, rippling along the clouds like threads of heat lightening until he can't feel himself falling asleep.

"Alberts," the sergeant whispers, touching Alberts' shoulder now. "You there?"

He gazes out beyond the trees, into the eastern sky. There is a slow-moving, single-engine plane up high and he can see the dim red light on the end of its wing like another planet passing the earth. The white light from the flashers reflects against a few scattered clouds.

"What's the matter?"

The sergeant straightens up and crushes his coffee cup in his palm. "You just kept staring. You okay?"

"Yeah—yes." He sweeps a hand in the direction of the search. "They find something?"

The sergeant shakes his head. "No I.D. Picture of some young girl, but that's it." The sergeant tosses his cup onto the street, then looks back at Alberts. "I hate these kinds," he says, screwing up his eyes. "Might take weeks before anyone realizes he's missing—maybe months before we even find out who he is. I bet there isn't an ounce of history at the department on this kid."

Alberts stares up at the sergeant. "He must have a name, some background information," he says, trying to appear somewhat composed. "What about his parents? He's just a kid. Someone should come for him. I've yet to see anyone not come for a body."

The sergeant chews the inside of his lip, makes a smacking sound with his tongue, holds his hands up, a supplicant. Alberts understands. Maybe some friends of the boy will show up at the morgue in a few days and say, "Yeah, that's Timmy," or, "Yeah, that's Bill," turning their faces from their friend, trying to light cigarettes with quivering hands. Or the father will arrive at the morgue. He'll stand at the side of the examining table and move a hand to his son's face, allowing the shadow of his finger to loiter over the black eyes and bruised cheek. He might nod and think of the last time he saw the kid—at a barbecue drinking a beer, talking to some pretty girl from down the street.

After a while Alberts watches as crime scene technicians zip the boy's body in a black body bag and gently load it into the ambulance, thinking this is the sum of all that the kid will be. A brief and unremarkable history.

Later, officers pack up their gear and leave. Silence returns to the scene. A cricket starts to chirp, then a few more, until a symphony of night sounds emerges above Alberts as he takes down the yellow tape, the night swallowing the infrequent swish of car tires on the overpass of I-75.

Alberts walks over to the outlined area where the boy was found. He crouches near the dirt shoulder and peers down at the blood that's dried on the sand and gravel. Then he pushes his thumb deep into the soil until grains of bloodied dirt squeeze up under his nail. He makes ravines and hills without any definition, just humps in the earth that will wash away with the next rain, become flattened by a passing car, or get smoothed over by a plow following a winter storm. He continues probing and shaping the loose earth, until a feeling of emptiness seeps into his chest as if carried by the stale air that funnels down his lungs with each breath. He stops digging, clenches a fist against his sternum and waits for the hollowness to subside into a dull ache.

He opens his eyes and stares down at the dirt. Tomorrow nothing will be left of the boy's life, he thinks to himself, pushing again into the fine bits of rock. He thinks of his father, of his lifetime of work and how the dead boy brings back the memory of the old man, one that fades as the years press on. But he knows he will never forget. Even distance and time can't erase one's history, now matter how small and immeasurable it may be.

The Bluff

They walk along the road that rims the bay. He follows behind, watching her small hips swing back and forth in her jeans. Through the trees to the right, he can see the broad limestone formation that surrounds the town below. After half a mile, she looks back over her shoulder and says, "Why can't you be this slow when we make love?"

He picks up a small stone and tosses it at her, making sure to aim to the left of her body, but the stone skips along the ground, banks sharply off a twig and arcs toward her feet. She laughs, but a moment later it erupts into a scratchy cough that causes the folds in her t-shirt to ripple along her back as her body trembles. He trots over to her; she raises a hand without looking at him and he stops. Finally she nods and moves on, stepping on the stone he'd thrown and increasing her pace until she finds the path entrance marked by a green highway pole hammered into the ground. Coils of purple thorn bushes choke both sides of the path.

He follows her to the bluff and stands behind her after they reach the top. Heavy gusts blow inland, pressing her t-shirt against her body.

"Look," she says, pointing to a mass of brilliant white rocks at the mouth of the bay. Waves swell against the lower parts of the formation, then spill over the rocks as the water retreats.

"The big waves usually stop by the end of the summer," he says. "At least they used to. By then the water in the bay is low and the forest is dried up, if we haven't gotten much rain. Once I saw them come in during the winter, when I was a kid. I got a plastic boat for Christmas and I floated it out into the water one day and watched the waves overtake it on some rocks."

"Oh, you poor baby," she says in an exaggerated voice. She extends a hand to him. He squeezes it, then lets it drop to her side.

A mud-smeared police truck gurgles on Ridge Street below as it moves deliberately through town. The sign from Rexall Drugs has rusted out since the last time he's been home. Two of the orange letters have fallen off and now the sign reads Rexa rugs. "Sometimes the spring thaw makes the water rise," he says, gazing down at the town. "Everything's gonna slide right into the water some day. Ground's loosening up. See that dead tree down near the water?"

He aims a finger over her shoulder, showing her the spot. For a moment the wind picks up her blond hair and hurls it into a small chaotic web. A few strands flutter in front of his face and come to rest in his mouth.

"See how it's all brown and grayish with the roots sticking out like pipes?" he asks, spitting out her hair. "Five years ago that tree wasn't really that close to the water. Maybe four, five feet away. When I was in grade school, we'd do science projects in the spring. We'd measure the erosion of the playground because it backed right up to the lake, and we put up stakes at the edge of the water. After winter was over, we'd come back out and see how far the land had retreated."

"Some places have good winters," she murmurs. "I'm glad we got here before the snow. At State they had good winters, didn't they?"

"They were all right. Too much rain for me."

He inches forward but stops. It seems to him that he is always behind her, out of her vision, as if on purpose. After they hold each other in bed, she often turns over on her side with her back facing him so that she can fall asleep. Sometimes, before she became ill, following a party or a night at the bar, they would stagger into their apartment and make love wherever they were with the lights off—the living room, kitchen pantry, even in the small space where the furnace hums in the bathroom closet. Many times he wondered what this would have looked like from the outside, with their pants pulled down to their ankles, the moonlight casting their shadow on the linoleum floor.

"I'm glad we got away this weekend," she says now. "The air is so clean here."

"Early and late fall's the time to come up. We're lucky it's so warm out right now. When I was twelve, we had this massive forest fire—"

She turns to him. Her lips are dry, a faded color of pink, but he knows that if he kissed her right now they would still feel moist and undamaged. The deception of her body amazes him each time he looks at her.

"It burned thousands of acres. Took days for the fire crews to put it out. Weird things is, when the fire was getting closer to town, the waves started growing smaller, like the fire was causing the bay to evaporate. Maybe they used lake water to put it out."

"Sounds like it," she says.

He smiles but the corners of his mouth feel stiff and awkward. He turns away briefly and faces the path. He peers at the muddy ground, trying to organize his love for her at this moment, balancing it between the things he knows are good and the things he isn't sure of anymore, but the two ideas confuse each other. After she first became ill, he'd begun a ritual of waking when the 3 a.m. freight train rumbled past their apartment in Plymouth and rattled her porcelain horses on the shelves opposite their bed. He'd turn over and gaze down at her, thinking she looked like a little girl with her hands balled into fists clutching knots of the blanket close to her mouth. He'd lightly touch her temple with his pinky and measure her breathing by placing his palm in front of her nose or by pressing his ear close to her opened mouth. Sometimes he'd nudge her awake with his foot and watch her face as she rubbed her eyes open and asked, "What?"

"Sorry, hon. Had a bad dream," he'd whisper.

She'd close her eyes and drape an arm over her forehead. In those moments, he wished he could become a speck of air that got sucked into her body and traveled the tunnel of her nasal cavity, touching the walls with his fingertips, or float into the murky blackness of her lungs and see the dull yellow glow of her sickness. Every day at work, as he'd sit at his desk gazing out the window at the dark blue water of the Detroit River flowing by, he'd convince himself that this was the only way to understand what was happening to them. To imagine her condition as something concrete and easy to touch comforts him in the hours when her breathing sounds as if she's inhaling gravel late at night.

The first time they came to this bluff they were juniors in college. They'd made love, then stood naked on the bluff edge with their arms wrapped around each other's waist, staring down at the white lights that dotted the town. "I like this," she said, her head against his shoulder. "We should camp out here some night. Live up here by ourselves for a weekend. Our own bluff."

On that warm summer night her skin smelled vaguely of oranges. Years later after they were married, whenever she left for work, he would turn over in bed and still smell her on her pillow as if she hadn't gone. During their courtship his apartment contained a different odor, a scent which was his alone: musky, laden with sweat and old beer, tinged with the stench of cigarettes. Eventually his aroma became obscured by hers. Many times after she'd left for work, he'd stand in the doorway of the bedroom closet wearing nothing but his boxer shorts, inhaling the scent of her clothing until it was time for him to get dressed for work.

"I want to taste the water," she announces. Her eyes twitch, then open. He moves forward and wants to ask her how she feels, but stops short, realizing that she will simply shake her head, raise her hand toward him until the pain passes, and then tell him she is fine. Sometimes it's hard for him to witness her strength. Even a small, emotional breakdown might make her illness more real, concrete. A kind of weariness overtakes her in these moments: her brow creases and the skin around her eyes appears darker than usual.

"Maybe we should get back. Mom wants to have an early lunch," he says.

"Have you ever tasted the water?"

He thinks a moment. "Sure. When I was eight or nine, I had my tonsils taken out. After that, whenever I swam and swallowed some of the water, it reminded me of my surgery, kind of a metallic taste, like my mouth was made of steel."

"Let's go down to the shore," she says. "We haven't been there yet."

The wind blows hard, pushing her shirt tight against her body, displaying the outline of her rib cage. When she breaths, her round bosom rises and falls with each breath. He feels a desire to move closer and take her shirt off, but he knows he shouldn't.

He touches her hair. It's coarser from the treatments, but it feels stronger, sturdier. She has lost some of it, yet he still finds it comforting at night when she rests her head on his shoulder as they lie in bed together. Even now he wishes he could feel her tiny cold feet squeezed between his to keep warm or the sting of one of her toenails accidentally gouging his leg. When she falls asleep on his shoulder with her mouth open, saliva pools around her lips and seeps into his skin, but he doesn't wake her. In the shafts of pale moonlight that come through the aluminum blinds of their room, he often sees the shimmering wetness on her lips and he moves closer to kiss her.

"I'm going down there," she says now.

She clutches a piece of his shirt and lets go as she brushes past him. As she passes he can smell the faint odor of oranges and see every detail of her face—the lines around the corners of her eyes and the wrinkles on her forehead just below her hairline. Without makeup, her blue eyes appear naked and she looks older than thirty-four. There's still that confident shift of her hips when she walks, the same one he remembers from the first time they met at a party, though her bones are now more prominent. She walks hesitantly down the path, bending her back low for some branches and moving others out of her way with her hand.

"How 'bout doing it tomorrow," he calls after her. "Water's kind of rough." But she's moved out of sight, past the tall oak near the turn of the path. He stares into the purple thorn bushes, waiting for her response. A few seconds pass and he suddenly worries that he might not hear her response.

"Today," she finally calls.

He jogs down the path until he reaches the shore. To his right he can see smears of smoke from store chimneys in town and beyond that the brown hue of the forest studded with dark green pine trees. She stands on a carpet of white stones, hugging her body with her arms, watching the water at her feet.

"Let's go in," she says without turning around.

"Too cold. Even in the middle of the summer Superior stays below fifty degrees."

She walks to the edge of the water and kicks her tennis shoes off. With each big toe she peels her socks off.

"You're being a baby," she says and moves an inch or two into the lake. When her feet touch the water, her fingers splay apart and she catches her breath.

"I told you."

"It's not so bad," she whispers. She moves a few more inches into the water. "It gets better the longer your skin is used to it."

She walks out into the water until her jeans are soaked to her knees. She bends down, cups a handful of water, and flings it out into the bay as if presenting the lake with a gift.

"Coming in?" she asks. Her pale skin is bright against the dark cliffs behind her.

"I don't know. Let me think about it."

She dips her fingers back into the water and shudders from the coldness. When he stands behind her, she looks the same as she did the first time they camped out on the bluff. On that night, she laid on top of him, staring into his eyes. He couldn't see her face, but he remembers her white skin in the pale moonlight and the familiar curve of her back under his hand. She said, I can see your eyes so clearly, Justin. I can see your entire face.

"Justin," she says, her voice echoing against the formation and water. "It's really quite invigorating. Please come in, will you?"

He nods, then turns back and looks up at the bluff, thinking of how it would feel to be a child again, standing on the edge, staring down at the water with his father holding his shoulders so that he could lean forward, beyond the land, and gaze at the town and water below as if he hovered above everything like a leaf thrown into the air by the wind. When he had shouted hello, his voice swelled against the limestone formation and seemed to push the air forward; and when it bounced off the buildings in town, it came rushing back to him altered and more distant, in a way that made him uneasy.

She faces him now, holding a hand up as if to clutch his. He walks into the water a few feet without removing his shoes, believing, just for a moment, that there is no past or future to their lives, just the two of them standing in shallow water, invigorated by the coldness against their skin as if they'd encountered the big lake together for the first time.

"Oh, your shoes, they're getting wet," she says, pointing to his feet. Then she snatches his hand and squeezes it hard.

He places a palm on her chest between her breasts. Her face breaks into a smile.

"What are you doing?" she asks, blushing.

He nods at her.

"We could take our clothes off," he says, drawing her body closer to his.

In Autumn

He stands naked at the end of the dock. His body isn't used to the cold anymore and goose bumps rise on his sagging skin. Years ago, when Emmet stood against the autumn breeze early in the morning, he could feel the air rush over every pore of his body, making the short gray hair on the soft spot of his neck stand on end, sometimes freezing the follicles inside his nose solid. He read somewhere, maybe in Esquire or Time, that swimming in the cold water was good for the muscles and helps the mind relax. Now, as he watches the sun slowly recede into the horizon and the leaves skitter over the wood dock, Emmet isn't sure whether it's the water that sways and not his body.

He remembers the first time he stood staring down at the water, trying to find the courage to dive in. He gazed across the lake one early morning and watched the yellow reflection of light shimmer on the water from the cottage up on the bluff. An old couple, dressed in matching orange jogging suits, appeared in their yard and waddled over to the cliff edge to see what Emmet was doing, standing naked in fifty-degree weather. Emmet couldn't see their expressions, but he imagined their tight mouths and small eyes wrinkled up in disgust. From then on, whenever he stood on the dock, sometimes turning completely their way because he knew they couldn't see him clearly, they'd call the sheriff. But by the time the officer weaved his way-through the forest to the cottage, Emmet made sure he was seated inside beside the stone fireplace reading a book, or else working in his shop; on one occasion he even suggested that perhaps the couple was growing senile. His wife, Elisa, would vouch for him, nodding her head as she stood behind Emmet, the blue wad of her son's half-knitted sweater in her hands. Then the officer would turn, shake his head, and murmur his resentment for having to drive out to the lake this early in the morning.

Emmet considers the couple's death as his eyes roam the neglect of their cottage across the water—chipped flakes of green paint littering the ledges, upstairs windows shattered like broken eyeglasses, the rusted skeletons of lawn chairs teetering at the edge of the bluff. Perhaps there was a plane crash or car accident. Maybe a suicide pact. Maybe she became ill, passed away, then weeks later he died of a disease he refused to acknowledge, an affliction hidden in a dark and distant recess of his body. The immediacy of their death never weighed much on Emmet's mind; instead, it hovered like a lake fog early in the morning when he stood on the dock peering through the whiteness, trying to see if their lights had been left on.

He sees a man in a boat near a cove below the couple's cottage. Emmet and Benny used to fish that spot when Benny was a boy. Once, on a Sunday morning, just as the fog evaporated and orange shafts of sunlight pierced the sky,

Benny stood up in the boat. They were near the shore and the boy's line was tangled in a willow limb that slouched over the water. A raccoon had wandered down to the water's edge and stopped, its gray and black hair bristling at the sight of Benny and Emmet. Benny, standing in the boat, forgot his line and continued watching the animal. Though the lake is small, it's fed by underground springs from Lake Michigan; some parts are so black and deep that Emmet has yet to secure a reading on his depth finder. When Benny fell over and didn't rise to the surface, Emmet waited a few seconds without concern; the boy was a good swimmer, at least when he swam off their dock. After a moment, he yelled for Benny to quit clowning around and to swim on back to the boat. His voice echoed into the forest around him, mingling with the call of a distant crow flying somewhere above the tree tops. He could smell wet leaves along the shore as he searched the bank for Benny just in case he swam ashore. But no one was in sight.

Finally Emmet dove in. He rose to the surface, then dove again and again, until the fear and cold water had numbed his face and puckered his skin. The fact that his son could vanish so easily, so imperceptibly, into the steely black water two feet from the shore had never pressed down on him before, not even when Benny was a baby and loved to sit in the shallow of their beach, flicking drops of water onto his father and mother crouched beside him.

Emmet treaded water and considered ways he could tell Elisa, explain it to everyone. Inside his chest and stomach he felt a hollowness grow, as if he hadn't eaten for days. He began to weep as he hovered in the water and stared along the surface for his son. "Benny," he sobbed, looking back over the water before he pulled himself into the boat. When he looked up, he saw Benny sitting there, his Levis and sweater drenched, a meager, gap-toothed smile stitched across his mouth.

"I wanted to see what you'd do," Benny said, laughing at his father's attempt to hoist himself up.

"Damn it all, Benjamin," Emmet barked, squeezing the water from his purple sweater, his arms and legs trembling. "You don't do things like that. What's wrong with you!"

He leaned over and grabbed Benny by the shoulders, swore, shook the boy a few times, even told him he was grounded, until finally he grabbed Benny and hugged him with such intensity that his son lost his breath a moment. Benny continued smiling, his face still lit from his joke, until all Emmet could do was stare at his son, shaking his head. "Never again, Benny," Emmet said. "Never."

When he was nineteen, Emmet saw that smiling look on Benny's face again, the day he came home and announced that he had enlisted in the Army. He was going away to a land he had often asked his parents about on the nights they sat on the back porch after the evening news, drinking Stroh's beer and watching the sun sink into the horizon. Benny could never explain why he'd signed up. During gin rummy games, Emmet would look across the table at him, stare into his shadowed eyes, and wonder if he really knew his son at all. Perhaps Benny felt the same as he had when he'd joined during World War II—a feeling that things might pass by without his participation. To Benny, Vietnam was simply a drama televised each night, like the one he and his friends played as children, waving plastic rifles in the air and shouting orders as they ran around their house many years before. They pretended apples from the orchard in back were hand grenades until someone got clunked in the head.

Sometimes, as Emmet stood on his freshly cut lawn, or smoked his pipe on the back porch just before sundown watching neighbors' cars pass by on the street, he remembered Benny's figure before it disappeared into the shadowy door of the DC-10. Brown oil slicks scarred the white pavement. Benny, dressed in his new uniform, walked slowly into the fumes of jet fuel shimmering like heat in the air. He turned around, waved, then stood a moment peering blankly through the haze of Detroit Metro Airport at his parents for the last time, his blond hair brighter than at any other moment in his life. It was on those endless nights, standing outside on his drive and listening to the crickets chirp along the edge of his neighbor's yard, that Emmet wished his son had been born handicapped, deformed or with a physical imperfection like a heart murmur that would prevent him from going.

After the letter came, Emmet comforted Elisa, helped her to bed, and gave her warm milk at night. When she looked to him for comfort, he saw the relief in her green eyes. He could see Benny in her face, especially when she arched her eyebrows with questions neither of them could voice, and he found solace in her touch as she reached for him during the nights they couldn't sleep. Her skin had taken on a presence he had felt only once, just before their marriage, a softness and smell he equated with her fertility. Now, older, wrinkles starting to web on her body, Elisa had regained it. As they lay awake at night, her tears falling silently on his shoulder, Emmet wondered if her love was much more deeply rooted than his own. He couldn't cry in front of her. He felt weak, incapable, especially when undertaking the chores Benny had once performed without question: lugging the trash out on Tuesday nights, mowing the lawn, clipping the shrubs. Some nights Emmet would stand alone outside the garage, watching the sun set. He'd never been a religious man, but he liked to believe that his son was up there, somewhere above the sky in the dark emptiness of space, staring down at him and making things in his life more fluid and less inconsequential.

The years that followed Benny's death were filled with endless running. Trips to Australia, the Mediterranean, London, Switzerland. An Army brat, Elisa had been everywhere before, she and her mother following her father around the world, eating in the cafes of France and West Germany, skiing the alpine slopes of Switzerland. She showed Emmet the relief that could come from such an escape. They wandered the streets and alleys of foreign cities deep into the night like two drunken teenagers, clutching each other's arms.

When she got sick, Emmet couldn't imagine what had caused it. For days she didn't say what was bothering her, just as Benny had done when he shrugged off illness. But on the morning she didn't rise from bed, Emmet knew. Perhaps the water in Mexico had given her hepatitis; looking back, he remembered it was the one place she'd never been with her family. The disease bled her of all her energy, rusting her intestines from the inside out, until the day she died in the hospital, clutching Emmet's hand and whispering about the lake shore in northern Michigan where they were married, and the day Benny was born in the elevator of a high-rise in downtown Chicago.

He tried to pull himself together, to reel some sort of courage into his life. He would muddle through, he told himself, muddle through as before, a man half awake, so absorbed in his work now that his tool-and-die company grew, branching out across sixteen counties of Michigan and Ohio. His awareness of the things around him blurred and receded, as though he were continually drunk.

There were three women in the years after Elisa, divorcees who took trips with him on his yacht off Lake St. Clair and gave him sex on the deck in the hot sun. Women with pictures of their college-aged sons in their wallets, boys dressed in athletic jackets. Emmet had envisioned Benny attending college and perhaps playing football, or meeting his future wife. One day the boy may have even presented his father with a granddaughter, a brown-haired, green-eyed girl who resembled Elisa in all exactness of detail. Emmet could briefly suspend his losses with these women, but eventually, in the wake of their lovemaking, the smell of sex lingering on their bodies, he found himself empty and completely awake. He probed the tanned skin of their turned backs with his fingers, feeling the pock marks from childhood sicknesses like crevices on the moon. He wanted a sensation inside to arise, one he felt when Elisa was alive. But there was something hollow in his touch.

Now he stands naked, watching the dark water form circles and slap against the gray wood of the dock. The man fishing earlier near the cottage lurches in his boat toward Emmet. Emmet is sure he can be seen for what he is—an old man, white hair spiraled all over his body, stomach scarred with stretch marks, gray folds of skin beneath his eyes from hundreds of sleepless nights, his chest drooping like an old woman's. A man with cataract-clogged eyes, yellowing dentures, two houses and a yacht.

The boat glides toward the dock. The fisherman looks down into his lap, says, You *okay?* He places his rod behind him.

Yes, Emmet says.

The man glances around the lake, then at Emmet's cottage standing behind him, dandelions and buckwheat overgrown in the backyard, the dead oak trees creaking. A For Sale sign is plugged into the strip of dried-out grass that runs along the right side of the cottage. The faded wood rails of the porch are loose, and both ends sag to the ground.

Sir, it's only fifty degrees out. You must be freezing.

Emmet studies the man. He sees broad shoulders, a dark, three-day beard. The young man's small brown eyes are averted, squinting against the fading glare of the lake. He wears a college athletic jacket that reads Laker Hockey 19.

Who told you about this lake? Emmet asks.

The fisherman cocks his head, squints more intently at the trees and weeds behind Emmet, at the attic window, cracks radiating like a spider web. He scratches an ear, hesitates. *I, ah ... Well, my father did. He lives down in Traverse. We've fished here a few times.* The young man looks down at the water. *Sir, don't you think you should put something on? It's getting chilly out here.*

I haven't been here since 1968, Emmet whispers. He scans the lake. At the far end, near a cove with green willow trees that tilt precariously over the water, someone has erected the skeleton of a new cottage. *Long time,* Emmet mumbles.

The young man peers up at the sky, using his hand to shield his eyes. *Sir, you should put something on. Here,* he says, reaching for the white blanket draped about his knees, *Would you mind wearing this?*

Emmet stares down at the young man until he puts the blanket down. Emmet is looking for something in that face, perhaps an idea of what Benny might have looked like at his age, twenty-three, twenty-four.

The young man peers firmly into Emmet's eyes for the first time. *Sir, it's cold out here and it's only gonna get worse. Please, take my blanket. I'd hate to leave you like this.*

Emmet nods, smiling at the young man's generosity. He takes the blanket and with trembling fingers wraps it around himself. Then the young man rows on, past a thick stand of trees, the oars of his boat dipping into the amber spots of sun reflected on the water. He looks back over his shoulder a few times. The sky above is blue, growing bluer as the sun sinks into the horizon. Somewhere beyond the lake someone is burning leaves.

Emmet lets the blanket fall from his shoulders. He looks down at the water a moment, then dives in. At first the smack of cold water stings his bones, making him suddenly aware of all his movements. Then he opens his eyes underwater and sees the bits of mud hovering in the murky water like dust motes caught in a ray of light. Everything on the surface is blurred: the darkening sky, willow trees, the wooden dock. He reaches out to disturb a clot of weeds floating above him on the surface. The texture is soft, smooth, like wet toilet paper draped around his fingers, and when he squeezes, the weeds come apart in clumps and float away from him. He wants to stab a hand through the surface and bring these things underwater with him, but he holds his hands back. What remains of his life exists above the surface in a world of forests, lakes and cement, one that occasionally recedes from his vision as the days evolve into each other. Some times he experiences moments of great pleasure in his memories, which remind him of who he was, who he loved and the joy he took in the life he was fortunate to have achieved.

Finally he surfaces, letting the water rush over him, through his thin gray hair, up the crack of his collapsed aged rear. He treads water for a few seconds. His arthritic knees are steady, painless, and he thinks he could melt into water, become the current underneath, float somewhere slow and undemanding, to a place in the lake where leaves sit placidly upon the surface until their fragile skeletons have dissolved into the water.

Then, as he pulls himself from the lake, bones cracking, stiff fingers clutching the worn wood of the dock, he imagines the couple from the cottage across the lake looking down at him from their small bluff. Perhaps, wherever they are, they can still see him and are telling each other, *It's him, the one who used to fish with his son down in our cove, the one who swam naked.*

About the Author

Gary James Erwin was born in Detroit and grew up in Northville, Michigan, approximately 25 miles west of Detroit. His stories, essays and journalism have appeared in many journals and publications, including *Red Cedar Review, The Sun, Pebble Lake Review, The MacGuffin, Driftwood Review, Third Wednesday, 3288 Review* and *Santa Fe Literary Review* among others. His work has also earned two Pushcart Prize nominations and has been anthologized in *The PrePress Awards Volume II: Michigan Voices*. He attended Detroit Catholic Central High School, earned his undergraduate degree at Grand Valley State University and MFA from Western Michigan University. He is currently working on a novel. He lives with his wife, kids and critters in Clarkston, Michigan, and is the associate vice president of Marketing & Communications at University of Detroit Mercy.

Acknowledgements

Some of these stories appeared in slightly different form in the following journals and anthologies: "The Bluff" in *Santa Fe Literary Review;* "In Autumn" as "The Lurch" in The Sun; "Holes" as "Bullet Holes" in *Meat Whistle Quarterly* and *The PrePress Awards Volume II: Michigan Voices;* "Weather Patterns" in *Driftwood Review;* "Indian Pond" in *Red Cedar Review;* "The Rifle" in *Pebble Lake Review;* and "Exchange of Words" in *Adelaide Literary Magazine.* The author is grateful to the editors of these publications.